Fairy Tales by Hans Christian Andersen

Gill Books

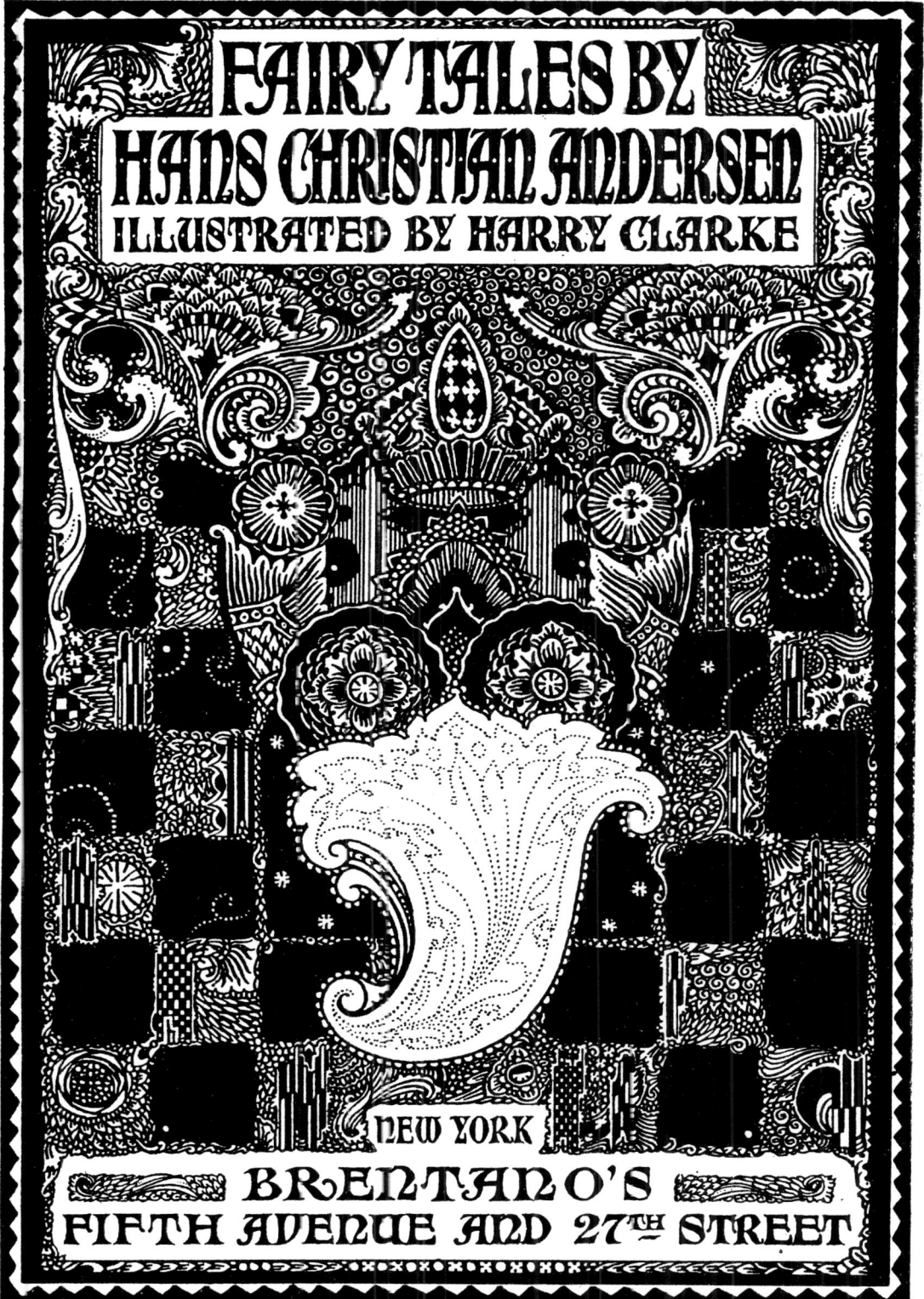

Gill Books
Hume Avenue, Park West, Dublin 12
www.gillbooks.ie

Gill Books is an imprint of M.H. Gill & Co.

Copyright © Teapot Press Ltd 2011

Copyright © NGI, introductory text, pages 6-13, 2011

ISBN 9780717150236

This book was created and produced by Teapot Press Ltd

Designed by: Tony Potter

Edited by: Elizabeth Golding, Helen Keith & Catherine Gough

Introductory text by: Niamh MacNally, Prints & Drawings, National Gallery of Ireland

Printed in China

This book is typeset in Bembo and Plywood Pro

All rights reserved.

No part of this publication may be copied, reproduced or transmitted in any form or by any means, without permission of the publishers.

A CIP catalogue record for this book is available from the British Library.

5 4

Contents

Introduction	6
The Tinder Box	14
Great Claus and Little Claus	22
Thumbelina	34
The Fellow Traveller	48
The Emperor's New Clothes	58
The Hardy Tin Soldier	64
What the Old Man Does is Always Right	70
The Storks	76
The Ugly Duckling	82
The Shepherdess and the Chimney-Sweeper	92
The Fir Tree	100
The Swineherd	106
The Snow Queen	112
The Nightingale	130
The Little Match Girl	142
The Elf Hill	146
The Little Mermaid	156
The Wild Swans	170
The Marsh King's Daughter	178
The Garden of Paradise	208
Original Paintings	217
Hans Andersen	222

INTRODUCTION

Harry Clarke's original illustrations for Hans Christian Andersen's Fairy Tales *at the National Gallery of Ireland*

Harry Clarke (1889–1931) was an artist of great genius, known both as a prolific stained glass artist and master book illustrator. He is generally acknowledged as Ireland's leading Symbolist artist. In whatever medium Clarke chose, he adeptly wove together an eclectic mix of influences to create his own unique vision. Book illustration offered the dualistic nature of his imagination great freedom. A close friend of the artist's, the playwright Lennox Robinson (1886–1958), described Clarke's graphic work as 'a mixture of the utterly beautiful and the macabre', drawn with 'a perfection of line, a minutia of detail'.[1] Decadence and refinement became a hallmark of his style, evident in his stylised compositions, populated by elegant figures in flamboyant costume with slender limbs and tapering fingers.

Hans Christian Andersen (1805–1875), born in Odense, Denmark, is one of the most celebrated and translated children's authors of all time. The author's fame stems from his renowned fairy tales and stories, written between 1835 and 1872, in particular 'The Ugly Duckling', 'The Little Mermaid', 'The Princess and the Pea', 'The Snow Queen', 'The Nightingale' and 'The Hardy Tin Soldier'.

Introduction

Inspired by the great tradition of the *Arabian Nights* and the Brothers Grimm, Andersen achieved worldwide recognition as the father of the modern fairy tale. However, the author was somewhat of a tortured soul, as in childhood he endured many hardships, suffered humiliations and taunts regarding his appearance, and experienced alienation among his peers due to his working-class beginnings. In relation to his talents, his ambition and supreme confidence was matched in equal measure by his desperate need for acceptance. Many of his compelling tales and stories empathise with those less fortunate. Andersen's colloquial writing style and use of wit often disguises the sophisticated moral teachings in his tales. As a shrewd observer of human nature, his stories teach us that appearances can regularly be deceptive, and highlight the fact that one can find beauty within even the most unlikely of characters. They also tend to poke fun at those who behave in a spoiled or conceited manner. His memorable tales have been widely illustrated by some of the best-known illustrators of the late nineteenth and early twentieth centuries – the Golden Age of illustration – including Britain's W. Heath Robinson (1872–1944) and Arthur Rackham (1867–1939), in addition to Denmark's Kay Nielsen (1886–1957) and France's Edmund Dulac (1882–1953).

Clarke's colour illustrations for Hans Christian Andersen's *Fairy Tales*, published in 1916, offer an exotic and original interpretation of the popular tales. Embellished with exquisitely crafted detail,

Clarke's illustrations enrich the much loved author's fairy tale world. Just as Andersen magically humanised toys and inanimate objects in his writings, Clarke brought to life Andersen's characters through a delicate blend of line, pattern and colour. The jewel-like colours, such as ultramarine blue, that suffuse the Andersen illustrations are reminiscent of the artist's work in stained glass. Dr Nicola Gordon Bowe, author of the 1989 landmark biography on Clarke, has noted that the glowing colours in his Andersen illustrations 'reveal the inspiration of the travelling scholarship he received in 1914 to look at medieval stained glass in France while working on this commission, as evidenced by the deep blues and rubies, and oranges and yellows offset with grisaille lacey greys'.[2] Bowe also points to the influences of 'Beardsley, the Rococo revival, the Ballet Russes, the Japanese print, [and] the Oriental miniature'.[3] The National Gallery of Ireland houses a first edition copy of Andersen's *Fairy Tales,* published by Harrap & Co. Clarke had given this book to Thomas Bodkin (1887–1961) as a gift in September 1916. Bodkin, a former Director of the National Gallery of Ireland (1927–1935), and great champion of the artist's work, admired his 'profound and independent imagination', in addition to his 'superb … technical accomplishment' and 'rare poetic feeling'.[4] He had been introduced to Clarke by one of the artist's most important patrons, Laurence Ambrose 'Larky' Waldron (1858–1923), the politician and eminent Dublin stockbroker.

In 1913, Harry Clarke, aged 24, who had recently finished his training at the Dublin Metropolitan School of Art, visited George Harrap, the principal London publisher of illustrated children's books. He presented him with a portfolio of his best illustrations for literary works by Coleridge, Keats, Pope, Synge, Yeats and Wilde. Harrap marvelled over the aspiring illustrator's mastery of line and colour and offered him, somewhat impulsively, his first major book illustration commission. Harrap reminisced: 'It is not often that a first book by

Introduction

Illustration from 'The Galloshes of Fortune'

an unknown and untried author or artist is given [this] distinction.'[5] This prestigious job, worth 200 guineas to the young artist, entailed producing 40 full-page illustrations for Andersen's *Fairy Tales*, published for deluxe and trade editions. Only 16 illustrations were to be in colour, the remainder in black and white, in addition to 16 decorative embellishments executed in pen and ink.

Clarke recorded in his diary of 1914 that each vibrantly coloured illustration generally took seven days to finish after an initial draft. He executed a good number of the illustrations in London, some in France and the rest in Dublin. Working scrupulously to a rigorous routine, Clarke completed the commission in Dublin in April 1915, around the same time that he commenced work on his first major stained glass commission for the Honan Chapel in University College Cork, completed in 1918. In the autumn of 1916, the book was published to great critical acclaim. Harrap described that, with this book, Clarke had 'interpreted the immortal tales with an imagination which penetrated the heart of his subjects and transmuted them into still more shining gold'.[6] This commission sparked a fruitful relationship between the Irish artist and the publishing house as Clarke would go on to illustrate numerous literary works for them, including: Edgar Allan Poe's *Tales of Mystery and Imagination*, 1919; Lettice d'Oyly Walters's *The Year's at the Spring*, 1920; Charles Perrault's *The Fairy Tales of Perrault*, 1922; and Goethe's *Faust*, 1925. The macabre imaginings of Clarke's Poe and Goethe illustrations perfectly complemented the more gruesome aspects of these dark stories. Clarke established his reputation with the Andersen illustrations and the Honan Chapel stained glass windows, and from that point on commissions poured his way.

In 1925, Clarke wrote that Brentano's of New York, Harrap's American publishing partners, took 'my originals for Hans Andersen

Introduction

… and they were shown in their bookshop in Fifth Avenue'.[7] The Brick Row Bookshop on East 47th Street, New York, also bought consignments of Clarke's original artwork and regularly exhibited them for sale. In retrospect this was extremely fortunate, as any original Clarke illustrations that remained in Harrap's London premises are believed to have been destroyed in the Blitz during World War II. The rarity of Clarke's illustrations is further compounded by the fact that a number of his haunting illustrations for S.T. Coleridge's 'The Rime of the Ancient Mariner', dated 1913–1915, were destroyed in a blaze at the premises of the publishing house, Maunsel and Co. Ltd., on Middle Abbey Street in Dublin during the Easter Rising of 1916.

Ten of Clarke's original colour illustrations for Andersen's *Fairy Tales*, prized for their pristine condition and rarity, were acquired by the National Gallery of Ireland in 2008, thanks to a generous gift from the Gallery's former Chairman, Lochlann Quinn, and his wife Brenda. The 10 watercolours in this gift illustrate the following magical tales: 'The Garden of Paradise'; 'The Hardy Tin Soldier'; 'The Snow Queen'; 'The Elf Hill'; 'The Swineherd'; 'The Shepherdess and the Chimney Sweep'; 'The Tinder Box'; 'The Travelling Companion'; 'The Wild Swans'; and 'The Nightingale'. These illustrations had been in America since the mid-1920s, where they had passed into the collection of Alfred Shands, an eminent orthopaedic surgeon, who died in 1981. He bequeathed them to his son Alfred R. Shands III of Louisville, Kentucky, who later decided to sell them on to The Fine Art Society in London. The 10 illustrations, which have now returned to Ireland, have significantly enhanced the National Gallery of Ireland's collection of works by the artist. Due to the delicate nature of works on paper, notably their susceptibility to the damaging effects of light, they cannot be placed

Hans Christian Andersen

Illustration from *The Galloshes of Fortune*

Introduction

on permanent display. However, they are accessible for viewing by appointment in the Gallery's Prints & Drawings Study Room.

In more recent years, only two other coloured Andersen illustrations that were published, apart from this series, came to light: 'The Little Robber Girl' and 'The Little Mermaid'. In 2010, the Gallery acquired 'The Little Mermaid' from a dealer specialising in book illustration in England. This now brings to 11 the number of original illustrations for Andersen's *Fairy Tales* by Clarke in the collection. The Gallery also houses a fine collection of over 60 drawings, watercolours and sketchbooks by the artist's wife Margaret Clarke (née Crilley) (1888–1961). In addition to working as an artist in her own right, she managed her husband's successful Stained Glass Studios on North Frederick Street, Dublin, after his premature death in 1931. Plagued by ill health for the majority of his working life, Clarke died in Switzerland from tuberculosis, aged just 41. Despite his short life, Clarke's level of industriousness and expertise is remarkable. Replete with intricate ornamental effects and theatrical flourishes, Clarke's exceptional graphic work and unparalleled stained glass designs continue to mesmerise and delight audiences to this day. The new photography carried out by the Gallery on all 11 illustrations in the collection, reproduced here in this book, gives a clear picture of the strikingly vivid colours Clarke applied nearly 100 years ago.

Niamh MacNally
Prints & Drawings Collection, National Gallery of Ireland

[1] Nicola Gordon Bowe, *Harry Clarke: His Graphic Art,* The Dolmen Press Ltd., Portlaoise, 1983, p.172.
[2] Nicola Gordon Bowe, *A Fairyland Mise-en-Scéne, Irish Arts Review,* Autumn 2008, Vol. 25. No. 3, p.1043.
[3] Nicola Gordon Bowe, *Harry Clarke - Ten Original Illustrations for Hans Christian Andersen's Fairy Tales,* The Fine Art Society, London, 2008, p.94. [4] Op.cit. no.1, p.415. [5] Op.cit. no.3, p.76. [6] Op.cit. no.1, p.327.
[7] Op.cit. no.3, p.14.

THE TINDER BOX

A soldier was marching down the road one day, with his pack on his back and his sword at his side, when he heard a voice croak, "You look like a brave soldier, who deserves to have as much money as he can carry!"

The voice belonged to an ugly, old witch.

"I should like that very much, old witch," said the soldier.

"Well, do you see that hollow tree?" said the witch, pointing.

"The money is down there. If you climb down inside I shall tie a rope around you to pull you back up again."

"But how will I find the money?" asked the soldier.

"At the bottom of the tree is a large hall with three doors leading off it. Unlock the first door and you will see a big chest in the

The Tinder Box

middle of the room. On top is a dog with eyes as big as teacups. Lift him off and put him on this white apron that I'm giving you. He will stay quiet while you take as many copper pennies as you can from the chest. The silver coins are in the next room, guarded by a dog with eyes as big as mill-wheels. Put him on my apron and he will be quiet while you take the money. If you want gold, go into the third room. The dog inside is a fierce dog, with eyes as big and round as towers. But put him on my apron and take as much gold as you like."

"But how shall I repay you, old witch?" asked the soldier.

"All you have to do is bring me back the old tinder box," said the witch. "My silly grandmother forgot it the last time she was down there."

The witch tied the rope around the soldier and gave him her apron. He dropped down inside the hollow tree and found himself in a large hall lit with a hundred lamps. There were three doors leading off the hall, each with a key in the lock. He unlocked the first door and there was the dog with eyes as big as teacups!

"Good boy!" he said, putting him on the witch's apron. He opened the chest and filled his pockets to the brim with copper coins. Then he put the dog back on the chest.

Next, he unlocked the second door. The dog with eyes as big as mill-wheels stared coldly at him. The soldier lifted him down on to the apron, threw away the copper coins and filled his pack and pockets with silver. Then he went into the third room. The dog's eyes, large as towers, were spinning.

"Good evening!" whispered the soldier, trembling. But he plucked up his courage and lifted the dog onto the witch's apron. The dog did not move. The soldier opened the chest and when he saw the gold coins inside, he threw away the silver and filled his pack, his pockets, his boots and his cap with gold.

"Pull me up, old witch," he called.

"Have you got the tinder box?" croaked the witch.

"Oh, I clean forgot," said the soldier, and picked it up from the floor. Then the witch pulled him up out of the tree.

"You've got your money," said the witch nastily, "now give me the tinder box."

"What's so precious about an old tinder box?" asked the soldier. "Tell me, or I shall cut off your head!"

"That's my business," snarled the witch. So the soldier cut off her head, tied up the money in her apron, put the tinder box in his pocket and walked into the town. As he was now rich, he stayed in the finest rooms at the best inn and ordered a splendid dinner. He bought fine new clothes and boots and looked like a grand gentleman instead of a poor soldier.

One day, he overheard two men discussing the king's beautiful daughter.

"The king keeps her locked in a stone castle because it was foretold that she would marry a poor soldier," said one man.

"I should dearly love to see her," thought the soldier.

The soldier was rich and lived well, but he was generous as well. He gave away as much as he spent until, in the end, he had only two pennies left. He moved into a tiny, dark attic. That night he remembered there was a stub of candle in the old tinder box. He struck the flint to get a spark and, to his amazement, the dog with eyes as big as teacups appeared. "What do you want, master?" he barked.

"So this is a magic tinder box," thought the soldier. "Bring me some money!" he ordered, and the dog disappeared. Moments later he was back, carrying a large bag full of copper coins.

The Tinder Box

" 'BUT HOW WILL I FIND THE MONEY?' ASKED THE SOLDIER"

The soldier now knew the value of the tinder box in his possession. He found that if he struck the tinder box twice, the dog with eyes as big as mill-wheels appeared, and if he struck it three times the dog with eyes as large as towers would immediately appear. He moved back to his fine apartment at once and bought new clothes and boots. He was soon surrounded by friends.

One night, the soldier lay thinking about the beautiful princess locked up in the great castle.

"Perhaps the tinder box can help," he thought, and he struck it once. The dog with eyes as big as teacups appeared and asked for his orders. "I want to see the princess," the soldier said. The dog vanished, but in a few moments it returned carrying the sleeping princess on its broad back.

The soldier gazed at the princess's lovely face and kissed her before the dog took her back to the castle. The next morning, the princess told the king and queen about her strange dream in which she had ridden on a dog and been kissed by a soldier. A lady-in-waiting was ordered to sit by the princess's bed that night, in case there had been any truth in the dream.

That night, the soldier sent the dog to fetch the princess again. With the lady-in-waiting chasing after the two of them, the dog carried the princess through the dark streets. It ran so fast that the lady-in-waiting could not keep up, but she saw them disappear into a large house. Thinking quickly, she pulled a piece of chalk from her pocket and drew a cross on the door to mark it.

Next morning, the king and queen set off with the lady-in-waiting and a crowd of courtiers to find out where the princess had been.

"It must be here," said the king, seeing a door with a cross.

"No, surely it is here," said the queen, pointing to another

The Tinder Box

"There sat the dog with eyes as big as teacups"

door with a cross. When they looked, they could see that every door in sight had a chalk cross on it. The clever dog had made sure that nobody would find its master.

That night, the queen tied a small silk bag filled with flour to the princess's waist and snipped a tiny hole in one corner. When the dog came to carry the sleeping princess to the soldier it did not notice the trail of flour that led straight to the soldier's door. Next morning, the king and queen discovered immediately where the princess had been. The soldier was seized and sentenced to death.

The soldier sat miserably in his cell wondering how to escape, especially as he had left the magic tinder box behind. Through the bars, he saw the crowds hurrying to watch his execution. He heard drums beating and soldiers marching. Suddenly a boy ran by so fast that one of his shoes flew off, hitting the wall under the cell window.

"Slow down," called the soldier. "The execution can't happen without me! If you want to earn four silver coins, go and fetch my tinder box." The boy ran off, and came back to pass it through the bars of the window. Then the soldiers came and marched the soldier through the streets and out of the town. A huge crowd surrounded the execution platform, and the king and queen sat on magnificent thrones. But before the executioner put the rope around his neck, the soldier called out, "Your majesty, please let me light my pipe for the last time!"

The king could not bring himself to refuse a dying wish, so the soldier struck the tinder box – once, twice, three times! Immediately there appeared the dog with eyes as big as teacups, the dog with eyes as big as mill-wheels and the dog whose spinning eyes were as large as towers.

"Save me from death!" yelled the soldier.

The dogs hurled the king and queen into the air and attacked the ministers. The terrified crowd cried out: "Stop them, good soldier. Have mercy. Marry the beautiful princess and be our king!"

The crowd carried the soldier shoulder-high and placed him in the royal carriage. The three dogs ran in front and the people followed, while the soldiers saluted.

The princess was freed from the great stone castle and she happily married the soldier. At the wedding feast, the three dogs sat at the table with the guests, staring with their enormous eyes.

Great Claus and Little Claus

Once upon a time, two men called Claus lived in the same village. One of them had four horses and the other just one horse. It was hard to tell them apart, so the people of the village called the man with four horses Great Claus and the other man Little Claus.

During the week, Little Claus was obliged to plough for Great Claus and to lend him his only horse. On Sundays, Great Claus helped out Little Claus by lending him his four horses. How excited was Little Claus! He cracked his whip over the five horses each Sunday, for they were as good as his for the day. As the church bells rang and the people listened to the priest, Little Claus was out in the fields cracking his whip and shouting, "Gee up, all my five horses!"

This didn't please Great Claus at all, "You mustn't say that!", he cried, "for only one of the horses is yours!"

But when no one was looking Little Claus would forget himself and shout again, "Gee up, all my horses!"

Great Claus was so upset that he screamed, "I beg you not to say that again, for if you say it again, I shall hit your horse on the head and he'll fall down dead!"

Little Claus apologised, "I'll certainly not say that ever again!" he said.

But as people walked past after church, and nodded "Good afternoon" to him, he became very proud of the horses he imagined to be his and cracked his whip again, and cried, "Gee up, all my horses!"

Great Claus was so mad, he said, "I'll gee up your horses!"

He grabbed his axe, hit Little Claus's horse on the head and it was dead in an instant.

"Oh my! Now I have no horse at all!" cried Little Claus. And he began to cry.

He then cut off the horse's skin and let the hide dry in the wind before putting it in a sack. He marched off to town to sell the skin. On the way, he went through a dark wood, where the weather became bad and he lost his way. It was nightfall by the time he found the right path and he was too far from home to return that night.

There was a large farmhouse close by the road. The shutters were closed, but he could see a light inside.

"Perhaps I could stop here for the night," he thought, then knocked on the door.

The farmer's wife opened the door, but she wouldn't let him in as her husband was away. She slammed the door in his face, so he found a little thatched outhouse. The straw thatch looked very inviting, but then he noticed a stork had made a nest on the roof.

Little Claus climbed up to the loft of the shed and made himself comfortable. From up here, he could peer into the farmer's dining room. He couldn't help but notice a huge table, laid with fine cloth and heaving with fish, meat and wine and a clerk sat ready for dinner.

The farmer's wife and the clerk were having a merry time, eating all the delicious food and drinking the wine.

"If only I could have some too!" thought Little Claus, as he stretched his head out of the window. "What a feast!"

He heard the clip-clop of a horse coming along the lane. It was the farmer's husband. He was a good man, but he had a real dislike for clerks! If ever he saw a clerk, he got very angry.

It was for this reason that the clerk had gone to visit his wife on this day, for he knew that the farmer would be out.

As soon as the pair of them heard her husband, they became frightened.

"Quick! into the empty chest," cried the farmer's wife, before hiding all the excellent food and wine. Little Claus watched the scene unfold before him, just as the farmer caught sight of him and said, "Hey! Who's that sleeping up there?"

Little Claus explained how he had lost his way and needed somewhere to sleep for the night.

"Well my fellow, come inside into the warm and have something to eat," exclaimed the farmer.

His wife received them both warmly and soon had a big bowl of hot porridge on the table. The porridge was fine, but Little Claus couldn't help thinking about all the delicious food that had been hidden.

His sack with the horse's skin was under his feet. He couldn't bear any more porridge, so he stood on the skin and made it crackle.

"Why, what have you in your sack?" asked the farmer.

"Oh, that's just a magician," answered Little Claus. "He says that we're not to eat porridge, but to feast upon the oven full of meat, fish and cake that he has conjured up!"

"Wonderful!" cried the farmer, as he opened the oven to find the delicious food that he imagined the wizard had produced.

The farmer's wife dared not say a word. Little Claus trod again upon his sack and made the hide creak.

"What does he say now?" asked the farmer?

"He says he has conjured three bottles of wine and that they are standing there behind the oven!" replied Little Claus. The two men drank the wine and soon became very merry.

"I'd like to see that magician of yours!" roared the farmer.

"Very well," said Little Claus and trod again upon the sack. As it crackled he said, "He tells me that he's very ugly and doesn't want to be seen."

"Well," said the farmer, "I'm not afraid. Pray, what will he look like?"

"He's the spitting image of a clerk!" exclaimed Little Claus.

"Ha!" said the farmer. "Now, that *is* ugly! I have to tell you that I can't bear the sight of a clerk!"

Little Claus stepped on his sack once again and the hide rustled. "My magician tells me that you may open the chest, whereupon you will find a demon that looks like a clerk!"

"Very well," said the farmer, "But you must hold the lid so he doesn't get out."

The farmer inched open the lid of the trunk containing the real clerk.

"Ha!" he cried and sprang backwards. "He looks just like our clerk – that was dreadful!"

So they sat up together late into the night, drinking all the wine.

"You must sell me your conjurer," said the farmer. "I'll give you a whole barrel of money."

"That I can't do," said Little Claus. "Think how much I can make out of this conjurer."

"Oh, I should so much like to have this magician!" pleaded the farmer and he went on begging.

After a time, Little Claus said, "As you have been kind to give me shelter for the night, I will let it be so. But I must have the barrel heaped with money."

"It's yours!" replied the farmer, "but you must take the chest away with you. I don't want it here another hour!"

Little Claus gave the farmer his sack with the dry hide in it, and got in exchange a barrel with money heaped up. The farmer also gave him a cart, on which to carry his money and the chest.

"Farewell!" said Little Claus and off he went with his riches.

On the other side of the wood there was a deep river with a fine new bridge. As he got to the middle of the bridge, he said out loud so that the clerk could hear, "Oh, what shall I do with this stupid chest? It's as heavy as lead and so I'll throw it in the river!"

He lifted the chest, as if to throw it in the river, when the Clerk screamed out, "No! Let me out!"

"Huh!" exclaimed Little Claus, pretending to be frightened. "He's still in there – if I'm quick I can throw him in the river and he'll drown!"

"If you let me out, I'll give you a barrel full of money!" yelled the clerk.

"Well, that's fine by me!" said Little Claus, and let him out of the chest right away.

The clerk ran to his house and fetched the barrel of money. Little Claus was soon on his way in his new cart, laden with riches.

"See, I've been well paid for the horse," he said to himself. He got home and tipped all the coins into the middle of the room. "That will upset Great Claus when he hears how rich I have become, but I won't tell him the whole story."

He sent a boy to Great Claus to ask for a measuring jug.

"Mmm..." thought Great Claus to himself, "what can he want this for?" So he smeared some tar under the jug so that whatever was to be measured would stick underneath. Sure enough, three brand new eight-shilling pieces were stuck to the jug when it was returned by the boy.

"What's this?" cried Great Claus. He ran off at once to see Little Claus. "Where did you get all this money?"

"I got it for my horse's skin," replied Little Claus.

Off went Great Claus to fetch his axe. He soon killed all four of his horses and cut off their skins to sell them in the town.

"Hides! Hides! Who will buy my hides?" he cried through the streets.

All the shoemakers and tanners came running to ask how much he wanted for them.

"A barrel of money for each!" said Great Claus.

"Are you mad?" they said. "Do you think we have money by the barrel?" All the tanners and shoemakers got together and decided that Great Claus was making fools of them and must be taught a lesson, so they beat him with strips of leather.

"WHERE DID YOU GET ALL THAT MONEY FROM?"

"Hides! Hides!" they called after him. "Yes, we'll tan your hide for you!" They chased after him until all were exhausted.

Great Claus reached his house and vowed to kill Little Claus.

At Little Claus's home, his grandmother had died. She had been harsh and unkind to him his whole life, but he was very sad nonetheless and carried her limp body to his warm bed in case the warmth would revive her. He tucked her up and sat in the chair beside the door and looked over her. As he sat there all night, the door opened and in marched Great Claus with his axe. He reached up and hit the grandmother on the head, thinking all the while that it was Little Claus in his bed.

"Do you see, Little Claus, that you shall not make a fool of me!"

Little Claus watched in horror as Great Claus attacked the already dead old woman. He sat silently and waited until Great Claus had gone. He dressed his grandmother in her Sunday best, borrowed a neighbour's horse and harnessed it to a cart. He propped her up in the front seat and off they trotted through the woods, stopping at an inn for refreshment.

The landlord was a hot-tempered fellow and very wealthy. Little Claus went inside the inn, leaving his grandmother propped up as if she were alive. The landlord poured a drink for Little Claus, then asked after his grandmother. Little Claus explained that she didn't want to come inside, so the landlord took her a glass of mead.

"Speak up, for she can't hear very well!" called Little Claus to the landlord as he walked out to the carriage.

"Here's a glass of mead from your grandson," said the landlord. The grandmother said not a word, so the landlord said again, "Here's a glass of mead from your grandson!" But she didn't reply. The landlord repeated himself three times again as loud as he could, getting crosser each time. At last he became very angry and threw the glass in her face so that the mead ran down her nose and she fell backwards into the cart!

"See what you've done!" screamed Little Claus. "You've killed her!" The landlord looked in horror!

"Dear Little Claus, this comes all of my hot temper!" said the landlord. "I'll give you a barrel full of money to keep quiet!" So Little Claus received another barrel of coins and the landlord buried the grandmother as if she had been his own.

Little Claus returned home and sent the boy again to fetch a measuring jug from Great Claus.

"What's this?" exclaimed Great Claus. "Have I not killed him?" And so he went over himself to see Little Claus with the jug.

"Now where did you get all that money from?" he asked as his eyes opened wide at the sight of it all.

"You killed my grandmother and not me," replied Little Claus, "and I have sold her for a barrel of money."

"That's good money for little work," said Great Claus. He hurried home, took an axe and killed his own grandmother. Then he put her in a carriage and drove to town to see the apothecary to ask if he would buy a dead person.

"Who is it and where did you get her from?" asked the apothecary.

"It's my grandmother," he answered. "I've killed her to get a barrel of money!"

"Heavens above!" exclaimed the apothecary, "You're raving mad and the constable will come for you!"

Great Claus unhitched a horse and galloped off as fast as he could to Little Claus's house.

"THAT'S A BAD FELLOW, THAT MAN"

"You've tricked me again!" shouted Great Claus. "But not again." He grabbed Little Claus and thrust him into a sack. "Now I shall go off with you and drown you in the river!"

They passed a church along the way, where they heard the sound of beautiful hymns being sung. Great Claus left the sack outside while he went in to hear a psalm. Little Claus was stuck tight.

"Oh dear!" he wailed, "I am too young to go to heaven."

An elderly cattle drover was passing by with his herd and heard him and said, "And I, poor fellow, am so old already, and can't get there yet!"

After a while, the elderly drover agreed to take the place of Little Claus, as he was anxious to get to heaven. Great Claus came out of the church and carried the sack to the river, whereupon he threw it into the water.

"Good riddance!" he cried and walked back along the track. But whom should he meet minding the cattle than Little Claus!

"But I just drowned you in the river!" he said with disbelief. "And how did you get those fine cattle?"

Little Claus explained patiently that when he fell to the bottom of the river in the sack, it immediately split open and a little mermaid appeared. She told him of a great white herd of cattle along the river and of untold wealth and happiness ahead. Whereupon she vanished and Little Claus found himself beside the river with a herd of magnificent cattle of untold value.

Great Claus listened intently and said, "Oh, you are a fortunate man! I too would like such a journey to meet the little mermaid and to find untold wealth. Will you help me into a sack and the river beyond?" he asked Little Claus. "Oh, and please add a rock to weigh me down so that I reach the bottom quickly."

"Of course, I will throw you in with great pleasure!" said Little Claus. So he bound him into a sack with a heavy rock and struggled down to the river, where he threw him into the running water.

The sack sank quickly and Great Claus was never seen again. Little Claus drove homeward with what he had.

THUMBELINA

Once upon a time, there was a woman who wished that she could have a child. She went to an old witch and said, "I wish I could have a child! Can you tell me how to get one?"

"I'm sure I can help," said the witch. "Take this barleycorn. It's not like the corn that grows in the fields, or like the corn that the chickens eat. Put it in a flower-pot and see what happens."

"Thank you," said the woman. She gave the witch twelve coins to pay her for the corn and she set off for home.

When the woman arrived home she planted the barleycorn. Instantly it grew into a beautiful flower. It looked like a tulip, but the leaves were closed tight like a bud.

"What a delightful flower," said the woman, and she kissed its yellow and red leaves. But as she kissed the flower it opened with a pop. In the middle of the flower, sat on the green velvet stamens, was the most delicate and graceful young girl. She was only half a thumb in height and so the woman named her Thumbelina.

The woman made a bed for Thumbelina out of a polished walnut shell, using violet leaves for the mattress and a rose leaf for a blanket. In the daytime, Thumbelina played on the kitchen table while the woman sewed. On the table sat a round, shallow vase of tulips and Thumbelina liked to sit on one of the tulip leaves that swam on the surface of the water. She would row from one side to the other, using two white horsehairs for oars. While she was rowing she would sing songs in the sweetest and most delicate voice that has ever been heard.

One night, as Thumbelina lay in her pretty bed, an old toad crept into the kitchen through a broken window pane. The toad was big, damp and very ugly. It hopped straight down onto the table where Thumbelina lay sleeping under her rose leaf.

"She would make a beautiful wife for my son," said the toad, and she took the walnut shell in which Thumbelina was sleeping and hopped with it through the window and down into the garden.

At the bottom of the garden there was a stream. The toad and her son lived at the edges of the water where the mud was swampy and soft. The son was very ugly and looked just like his mother. "Croak! Croak! Brek-tek-tek!" was all he could say when he saw the beautiful Thumbelina in her delicate walnut shell.

"Don't speak too loud or you'll wake her up," said the old toad. "She's as light as a swan's feather and she might run away, so we'll put her out in the stream on one of the big water-lily leaves. She's so small that to her it will seem like an island. Meanwhile, we'll decorate the house under the marsh that the two of you will live in."

Out in the stream there were lots of water-lilies with big green leaves that looked like they were floating on the water. The leaf furthest from the bank was the biggest of all and the old toad swam out and laid Thumbelina and the walnut shell on it. Thumbelina woke up early in the morning and when she saw where she was she began to cry. She was surrounded on all sides by deep water. The old toad was decorating a room for her new daughter-in-law with rushes and yellow weeds. When she had finished she swam out with her ugly son to the big green leaf on which Thumbelina sat. They wanted to take her pretty bed and put it in the bridal room before they took Thumbelina there. The old toad bowed before Thumbelina and said, "Here is my son; he will be your husband and you will live happily together in the marsh."

"Croak! Croak! Brek-tek-tek!" was all the son could say.

Then they took the little bed and swam away with it. Thumbelina sat all alone on the green leaf and wept. She did not want to live with the old toad and marry her ugly son. The small fish swimming in the water below had seen the old toad and heard what she had said. They stretched their heads up out of the water to see Thumbelina. When they saw how pretty she was they felt sorry for her having to marry the ugly toad. They gathered around the green stalk of the leaf, which held it in place in the middle of the stream, and gnawed at it with their teeth until it broke. The leaf swam away down the stream, taking Thumbelina far away from the toad.

Thumbelina sailed past many cities. Along the way all the little birds in the bushes saw her and said, "What a beautiful girl!" The leaf floated further and further down the stream until Thumbelina found herself in a new country.

A graceful white butterfly had been following her all the way, and finally it landed on the leaf. It liked Thumbelina and she was pleased to have it as a friend. She was happy to be far away from the toad and to be floating along the peaceful stream where the sun shone on the water and made it glisten like gold. She took off her stocking and tied one end around the end of the leaf. Then she tied the other end around the butterfly's middle. The butterfly flapped its wings so that the leaf glided much faster down the stream.

Suddenly, a huge beetle flew overhead and spotted Thumbelina. He flew down and clasped his claws around her waist, before flying off with her up into a tree. The green leaf went swimming off down the stream, taking the butterfly with it.

Thumbelina was terrified as the beetle soared up into the air. She was also worried about the poor white butterfly, which would starve if it could not free itself from the leaf. But the beetle didn't care. He landed on the biggest leaf of the tree, gave Thumbelina some sweet flowers to eat and told her that she was very pretty, even though she looked nothing like a beetle. Later, all the beetles living in the tree came to look at Thumbelina. "She's only got two legs! How horrible she is!" said one of the beetles.

"She hasn't got any feelers!" cried another.

"Her waist is too small. She looks like a human – how ugly!" said all the lady beetles.

Thumbelina was very pretty – even the beetle that had flown off with her could see that. But when all the others said she was ugly he started to believe it. The beetle told Thumbelina that he wanted nothing more to do with her and then he flew her down from the tree and left her all alone on a daisy. Thumbelina wept because she thought she was too ugly even for the beetles, which was a shame because she was the loveliest girl you could imagine and was as pretty and delicate as a rose leaf.

Thumbelina spent the whole summer living alone in the great wood. She wove herself a bed made from blades of grass and hung it up beneath a shamrock to keep off the rain. She ate the honey from inside the nearby flowers and she drank the morning dew from the leaves. Summer and autumn came and went, and soon it was winter. It was a long, cold winter and all the birds which usually sang softly in the trees flew away. The trees and flowers shed their leaves and the shamrock under which Thumbelina lived shrivelled up until it was just a withered yellow stalk. Thumbelina's clothes were torn and she was so cold that she nearly froze. One day, it started to gently snow, but because Thumbelina was so frail and delicate, and only an inch high, every snowflake that fell on her was like a shovel of snow hitting her. She wrapped herself in a dry leaf, but it tore in half and didn't keep her warm.

Close to the wood there was a huge cornfield. The corn had been cut short many months before so all that was left were stumpy stalks poking out of the frozen ground. But for Thumbelina the stalks were like a great forest. She wandered through it, trembling with cold, until she reached the door of a field mouse. The field mouse's home was warm and comfortable. It had a whole room filled with corn, a wonderful kitchen and larder full of food. Poor Thumbelina stood at the door like a beggar and asked for a little bit of barleycorn because she hadn't eaten a single morsel for two days.

"You poor creature," said the field mouse, "come into my warm home and I'll make us both some dinner." The field mouse was kind-hearted and so she shared her food with Thumbelina.

The field mouse liked Thumbelina and said, "You can stay with me this winter if you would like to, as long as you keep the house clean and tidy and tell me lots of stories."

So Thumbelina agreed to stay and they had a wonderful evening together.

Thumbelina

"She took her girdle and bound one end of it round the butterfly"

"Soon we're going to have a visitor," said the field mouse the next day. "My neighbour, the mole, visits me once a week. He is richer than I am, has a bigger house and has fur like a beautiful black velvet cloak. If you married him you would never be hungry or cold again, so remember to tell him the most charming stories you know."

So the mole visited every week. Each time, the field mouse told Thumbelina how rich and clever he was, how his house was twenty times bigger than hers, and that he did not like the sun or flowers because he had never seen them. But Thumbelina didn't care about the mole's wealth and she didn't want to marry him.

Every time the mole visited, Thumbelina had to sing. She sang "Ladybird, Fly Away" and "When the Parson Goes into the Field", and her voice was so beautiful that the mole fell in love with her, though he was a quiet man and he did not tell her.

The week before, the mole had dug a long tunnel through the earth from his house to field mouse's door. He told Thumbelina and the field mouse that they could walk in the tunnel as often as they liked. The mole warned them that inside there was a dead bird, but that they need not be frightened of it – it had died only a short time before and had been buried there.

The mole took a piece of rotting wood and lit it to make a torch, which he carried in his mouth while he led them down the tunnel. When they reached the bird, the mole used his big nose to make a hole in the earth so that sunlight shone down into the tunnel. In the middle of the tunnel lay a dead swallow. His beautiful wings were pressed up close to his side and his head was tucked beneath his feathers. He looked as though he had died from the cold. Thumbelina was sad; she loved all the birds that sung and twittered their pretty songs during the summer. But the mole kicked the swallow with his crooked legs and said, "He can't sing any more! It must be miserable to be a bird – they have nothing except their songs and they starve when winter comes. I'm glad none of my children will grow up to be birds."

"Yes, you're right. You are a clever man," observed the field mouse. "What good is a song when the winter comes? Birds just starve and freeze."

Thumbelina stayed silent, but when the others' backs were turned she knelt down, moved aside the feathers covering the bird's head and kissed him gently.

"Maybe it was this bird who sang such sweet songs during the summer," she thought. "How happy his songs made me, the poor beautiful bird!"

The mole closed up the hole to stop the daylight shining in and then he guided the ladies home. That night, Thumbelina could not sleep. She got out of bed and wove a large beautiful blanket out of hay, which she carried down the tunnel and spread over the dead swallow. She had brought some flowers with her from the field mouse's room and she laid down the soft petals all around the bird so that he was lying on soft ground.

"Farewell, pretty bird!" she said softly. "Farewell and thank you for your beautiful songs in the summer, when the trees were green and the warm sun shone on us." With that, she laid the bird's head upon her heart. Suddenly, as if by magic, the bird came alive. He had not been dead, but had been lying there so cold that he could not move. Now that Thumbelina had warmed him, he had awoken from his cold slumber and come back to life.

In the autumn, all the swallows fly away to warm countries. But if a bird is late it becomes so cold that it falls to the ground, as if it were dead. It lies forever where it fell and before long it is buried in snow.

Thumbelina was so startled that she jumped. The bird was much larger than her! But she was brave and she laid the soft petals closer to the poor bird. She brought a leaf, which she had used as a blanket on her bed, and laid it over the bird's head.

The next night she crept down the tunnel again. Now the bird was wide awake, but he was so weak that he could only open his eyes to look at Thumbelina for a moment. "Thank you for warming me, you pretty child," he said. "Soon I will be strong enough to fly around outside in the warm sunshine."

"Oh no," she said, "it's freezing cold outside and the ground is covered in snow. Stay here in your warm bed and I will look after you."

Thumbelina brought the swallow a flower petal filled with water to drink. He told her how he had torn one of his wings on a thorn bush and so had not been able to fly as fast as the other swallows, which had flown away to warm countries for the winter. Eventually, he had fallen to the ground, but that was the last he could remember. He had no idea how he had ended up in the mole's tunnel.

The whole winter long, the swallow stayed in the tunnel while Thumbelina nursed him back to health. Neither the field mouse nor the mole cared because they did not like the poor swallow. Soon spring came and the sun warmed the earth again. Thumbelina opened up the hole in the ceiling of the tunnel so that the sun could shine its golden warmth onto the swallow. He said farewell and asked Thumbelina to go with him on his journey; she could sit on his back and they would fly far away into the green wood. But Thumbelina knew that the field mouse would be sad without her, so she decided to stay.

"I'm afraid I can't, dear swallow," said Thumbelina.

"Farewell, farewell, you kind girl!" said the swallow, and he flew out into the sunshine. Thumbelina watched him fly away and tears welled in her eyes. She was very fond of the swallow and would miss him dearly.

"Tweet-weet! Tweet-weet!" sang the swallow as he flew into the forest.

Thumbelina wished she could go out into the warm sunshine, but the corn in the neighbouring field had once again grown into a great wood and she was only an inch high.

"The mole has proposed and you are now betrothed, Thumbelina," said the field mouse that evening. "A wealthy man proposing to a poor child like you – isn't that wonderful? You must start making your outfit! You'll need both woollen and linen outfits, for you will need a large wardrobe if you are going to be the mole's wife."

So Thumbelina had to turn the spindle and the mole hired four spiders to weave for her day and night. He visited every evening and each time he told her that when the summer had ended, and the sun no longer burned the ground as hard as stone, they would get married. But Thumbelina was not happy. She found the mole tiresome and she wished that she could see the swallow again. Every morning when the sun rose, and every evening when it went down again, Thumbelina crept out the door and looked up at the sky. When the wind blew, the corn in the field was parted so Thumbelina could glimpse the blue sky and could see how bright and beautiful it was outside. But the swallow did not come back; he had flown far away into the green forest. When autumn arrived, Thumbelina had her outfits ready.

"In four weeks you'll be married," said the field mouse.

But Thumbelina wept and said that she would not marry the mole.

Hans Christian Andersen

"She should be queen of all the flowers"

"Nonsense," said the field mouse, "don't be stubborn, or I'll bite you with my white teeth. He is a fine man and you will marry him. Even the queen does not have fur as black and velvety as his, and his cupboards and cellars are full. You should be thankful for your good fortune."

Soon it was the day of the wedding. The mole had come to fetch Thumbelina. She was to live with him deep in the earth and never come out into the warm sunshine that he hated so much. Poor Thumbelina was full of sorrow. At least at the field mouse's home she had been able to see the sunshine from the doorway, but now she must say farewell to it forever.

"Farewell, bright sun!" she said, stretching her arms out towards it. She walked a little way from the house, for now the corn had been harvested and only the stumpy stalks were left in the field. "Farewell!" she repeated as she stroked a little red flower that grew there. "Say hello to the swallow for me, if you see him."

"Tweet-weet! Tweet-weet!" a voice suddenly sounded above her head. Thumbelina looked up; it was the swallow! When he saw her he was very glad. Thumbelina told him how she had to marry the ugly mole and that she must live deep under the earth where the sun never shone. Then she wept and wept.

"Winter is coming now," said the swallow, "and I am going to fly to the warm countries. Will you come with me? You can sit on my back and we'll fly over the mountains, far away from the ugly mole and his dark rooms. It is summer there and there are lots of lovely flowers. Fly with me Thumbelina, so I can repay you for saving my life when I lay frozen in that dark, earthy tunnel."

"Yes, I will go with you!" said Thumbelina, and she climbed onto the swallow's back. She put her feet on his outstretched wings and tied her belt to one of his strongest feathers. Then the swallow soared up into the sky. He flew above the forest and over the sea and high up over great mountains where the snow always lies.

Thumbelina felt cold so she snuggled beneath his warm feathers until only her head was left uncovered, and then she admired all the beauty beneath her.

Finally, they arrived in the warm countries. The sun shone far brighter than it does here and the sky seemed twice as high. On all the hedges there grew beautiful blue and green grapes, and oranges and lemons hung in the woods. The air smelled sweet and soft, and children played with the butterflies in the meadows. But the swallow flew further still and the land became even more beautiful. Next to a glistening blue lake, beneath glorious green trees, there stood an ancient palace of dazzling white marble. Vines spiralled around the marble pillars and on top of the pillars there were many nests. The swallow lived in one of these nests with his family.

"This is my house," said the swallow, "but you shouldn't live here. It's not finished and you wouldn't be happy in it. Choose one of the splendid flowers that grow nearby and I will put you on it. Then you can have everything the way you want it to be."

"Wonderful!" cried Thumbelina, and she clapped her hands with joy.

On the ground there lay a great marble pillar that had fallen and broken into three pieces, and between the pieces grew the most beautiful white flowers. The swallow flew down with Thumbelina and she sat upon one of the broad green leaves. But what a surprise Thumbelina had! In the middle of the flower sat a little man, as white and transparent as if he had been made of glass. He wore a gold crown on his head and he had bright white wings on his shoulders. He was the angel of the flower and he was no bigger than Thumbelina. In each flower there lived a little man or woman, but this man was king of them all.

Thumbelina

"How beautiful he is!" gasped Thumbelina.

The king was very frightened of the swallow because he was such a gigantic creature compared to him. But when he saw Thumbelina he was delighted; she was the prettiest girl he had ever seen. He took off his crown, placed it on her head and asked her name. Then he asked if she would be his wife and be queen of all the flowers. The king was very different to the ugly toad and the mole. He was charming and kind, and so Thumbelina said, "Yes". Out of every flower came a man or woman and each one was a delight to behold. Each brought Thumbelina a present. The best gift was a pair of beautiful wings, which had belonged to a great white fly. They were fastened to Thumbelina's back so that she could fly from flower to flower. Everyone rejoiced and the swallow sat above them in his nest. He had been asked to sing the marriage song, and when the wedding day came he sang as well as he could. But in his heart he was sad, for he was so fond of Thumbelina that he did not want to leave her when it was time for him to fly back to the green wood.

"You shall no longer be called Thumbelina," said the king on the wedding day, "you are too beautiful for it. From now on, we will call you Maia."

"Farewell, Farewell!" cried the swallow with a heavy heart, and with that he flew away from the warm countries, far away back to the green wood. There he has a little nest above the window of a man who tells fairy stories. To him the swallow sings sweet songs of "Tweet-weet! Tweet-weet!" and it is from him that we have this story.

THE TRAVELLING COMPANION

Johannes sat quietly holding the hand of his dying father. Suddenly, the old man opened his eyes and said, "You have been a good son, Johannes. God will always help you." With that he closed his eyes and died, leaving Johannes all alone in the world.

The sun shone gloriously on the day of his father's funeral. Johannes thought, "I will try always to help people so that one day I will be able to join my father in heaven." Next morning he set out into the world, but first he stopped beside his father's grave to say a prayer and wish him goodbye.

That night, Johannes slept under the stars in a hayrick as comfortably as if he were a king in his bed. In the morning, he heard bells ringing and followed the villagers to church. He noticed that some of the graves in the churchyard were neglected so he tidied

The Travelling Companion

them up, hoping that other people might look after his father's grave in the same way.

By the church door stood an old beggar, leaning on a crutch. Johannes gave him what little money he had and set out again on his journey. As night began to fall, a wild and violent storm blew up. On a nearby hilltop was a small, lonely church, and he went inside to shelter. He settled down in a corner and fell fast asleep. A noise woke him in the middle of the night. The storm was over and the moon shone through the windows, lighting up an open coffin in the middle of the church. Two men were lifting the body out of the coffin.

"What are you doing?" cried Johannes. "In God's name, let him rest in peace."

"He owed us money!" said the wicked men. "So we are going to throw him out to lie in the churchyard like a dog!"

"Take my money," said Johannes. "I don't need it. God will look after me." And he gave the villains all the money he had and gently lifted the body back into the coffin.

Before dawn, Johannes set off again through a dense, black forest. He was not afraid, even when the moon lit up tiny elves dancing among the leaves and speckled spiders spinning gossamer webs in the hedges. The sun was rising when he heard a man's voice call out, "Hello there, my friend. May I keep you company during your travels?"

"I should like that," said Johannes, and the two walked on together.

At mid-morning they sat down under a tree to rest when an old woman carrying a bundle of sticks hobbled by. Suddenly she slipped and fell, breaking her leg. Johannes rushed to help her while his fellow traveller opened his knapsack and took out a box of ointment.

"This ointment will mend your leg and make it stronger than before," he said to the old woman. "All I ask in return is three of your willow sticks."

The old woman gladly agreed, and the stranger rubbed on the ointment, making her leg as good as new. Johannes and his fellow traveller went on their way and stopped at an inn for the night. Inside, a crowd was watching a puppet show. The show was just coming to the most exciting part when a bulldog suddenly jumped up and snatched one of the puppets in its jaws.

The fellow traveller rubbed onto the broken puppet the same ointment that had cured the broken leg. At once the puppet was mended and was even better than before. Now it moved and danced without strings.

In the middle of the night, people in the inn were woken by loud groans coming from the puppet theatre. All the other puppets were crying because they too wanted to be able to move by themselves!

"Please rub your ointment on all my puppets," begged the puppet-master, and he offered the traveller all the money he had. As soon as the puppets were smeared with ointment they began to dance, which made everyone else want to dance too! Johannes' fellow traveller would not take the puppet-master's money, but in return he asked him for his sword. Early next morning, he set out with Johannes for the mountains. They climbed higher and higher, and Johannes was so entranced by the sight of the world around him that his eyes filled with tears and he said, "I have never seen such beauty! What a wonderful world we live in."

As they stood gazing at the scene, they heard a swan singing its dying song in the air above. Then its voice grew faint and it dropped to the ground.

The Travelling Companion

" 'I AM GOING OUT INTO THE WIDE WORLD TOO,' SAID THE STRANGE MAN"

"Two beautiful white wings are worth money," said the fellow traveller, and he cut off the dead swan's wings with his sword.

The two men crossed the mountains and descended to a large city. They stopped at an inn where the landlord told them about the good king who ruled there and his wicked daughter. She was a witch and responsible for the death of hundreds of young men who had tried to win her hand in marriage by guessing her thoughts.

"What a wicked princess!" said Johannes. "She deserves to be beaten."

Suddenly they heard cheering outside the inn. The princess was riding by on a snow-white horse. She wore a gold crown made of tiny stars and a cloak of butterfly wings, and was accompanied by twelve beautiful ladies dressed in white silk and carrying golden tulips. When people gazed on the princess's dazzling beauty they forgot how bad she was, and as soon as he saw her Johannes fell in love with her.

"I will go to the palace and win her. I am sure I can guess what she is thinking," he thought.

The king welcomed Johannes to the palace, but when he heard that he wanted to win his daughter he began to sob, "I beg you to think again," he said. "You will end up like the others. Look."

He led Johannes into a garden where a horrifying sight met his eyes. From every tree hung the skeletons of kings' sons, and in the pots where flowers should have bloomed were piles of grinning skulls. But Johannes was not put off, and when he saw the princess again he thought she was lovelier than ever. She told him to return the next day so that the whole court could judge the guessing. If he succeeded, he would return twice more, but if he failed his head would be cut off.

When Johannes told his fellow traveller that he was going to the palace the next day, the man shook his head and said, "Poor, dear

Johannes. Tonight we must enjoy ourselves for I fear tomorrow I shall be crying."

So they spent the evening talking and drinking wine until Johannes was so sleepy that he went to his bed. While he slept, the fellow traveller fixed the white swan's wings to his shoulders and picked up the largest of the sticks given to him by the old woman. Then he opened the window and flew over the town to the palace. He hid under the princess's window until it opened and she flew out on black wings and headed for a high mountain. The fellow traveller made himself invisible and flew after her, hitting her with his stick.

"It must be hailing," said the princess as the blows stung her.

When she reached the mountain, a door opened in its side and she entered, followed by the invisible traveller. They walked down a long passage lit by glittering spiders and reached a hall, where red and blue flowers grew from the walls, glow-worms illuminated the ceiling and bats hung upside down, flapping their wings. A wrinkled old wizard sat on a glass throne supported by the skeletons of four horses beneath a canopy of deep-red cobwebs. He kissed the princess and she sat beside him while a strange orchestra began to play. Huge black grasshoppers chirped, an owl beat out a rhythm with its wings and goblins pranced around the room.

The princess told the evil wizard that another young man hoped to win her, and asked him what thought she should make him guess the next day.

"Choose something easy that he will never think of," said the wizard.

"Think of one of your shoes. He will never guess that. Then you must have him beheaded and bring me his eyes." The princess promised to do so and said goodbye. The invisible traveller flew close behind her all the way back to the palace, hitting her with the stick.

Next morning the fellow traveller told Johannes that he had dreamt about the princess's shoe and that he felt sure this was the answer to the riddle.

"I will trust in God," said Johannes, "but her shoe sounds as good a guess as any."

The palace was crowded with people. The judges sat with their heads propped on cushions and the king sat wiping the tears from his eyes. When the princess appeared she seemed more beautiful than ever. She looked at Johannes and said, "What am I thinking of?"

"Your shoe," replied Johannes straight away.

The princess turned as pale as chalk and the king leapt up joyfully.

That night, while Johannes slept, the fellow traveller again flew behind the princess to the mountain, this time beating her with two willow sticks. When the princess asked the wizard what to think of next he suggested her glove. In the morning, the fellow traveller again told Johannes he had had a dream, this time about the princess's glove. When Johannes guessed correctly a second time the whole court jumped for joy, but the princess said nothing.

On the third night the fellow traveller took three willow sticks and his sword and flew towards the palace. A storm was blowing so hard that tiles from the roofs were flying everywhere, and the skeletons in the garden clanked their bones as they shook. The princess, looking deathly pale, flew from her window and headed for the mountain through the stormy skies, followed by the fellow traveller thrashing her with all three sticks.

Inside the mountain she told the evil wizard that Johannes had guessed right a second time.

"He will not do it a third time," snarled the wizard, "unless he is a greater magician than I am."

The Travelling Companion

"Let him have his head cut off"

He took the princess's hands and they danced to the music of the strange orchestra. When it was time to return to the palace the wizard flew back with the princess. The invisible traveller stayed close behind, hitting them both with the sticks.

"What a violent hail-storm," said the wizard. Then to the princess he whispered, "Think of my head." The princess slipped in through her window. The wizard turned to fly back, but the fellow traveller grabbed his beard and cut off his head with the sword. Next day the fellow traveller handed a bundle to Johannes.

"Do not open this until the princess commands you to tell her what she is thinking of," he said.

The court was more crowded than ever when Johannes appeared before the princess for the third time.

"What am I thinking of?" she asked him sternly. "Remember, your life is at stake!"

As everyone in the court held their breath, Johannes picked up the bundle. Slowly he unwrapped it, and out rolled the head of the evil wizard. The princess sat as still as a statue and did not say a word. At last she stood up and held her hand out to Johannes, saying, "We shall celebrate our wedding this evening."

"At last," cried the old king, "my dearest wish will be fulfilled." The whole court shouted and cheered.

But the fellow traveller knew that the princess was still a witch, and the dead wizard's spell over her had to be broken. He gave Johannes three swan's feathers and a small bottle of magic drops and told him to mix them in a bath of water.

"When the princess is about to get into her bed, push her gently so that she falls into the bath. To break the spell and make her love you, you must dip her head under the water three times."

The Travelling Companion

Johannes did as he was told. The princess screamed when he pushed her under the water the first time and struggled back up to the surface in the shape of a black swan. Johannes pushed the swan back under the water a second time, whereupon she rose again to the surface. This time, the swan had become white with a black neckband. But Johannes pushed her into the water a third time and finally she was changed back into the beautiful princess. She was far lovelier than before and rose with tears in her eyes, thanking him for having broken the evil spell that bound her.

The next morning, the crowds gathered round the new prince and his princess, cheering and congratulating them. Last of all came the fellow traveller, with his stick in his hand and his knapsack on his back. Johannes hugged him lovingly, begging him to stay with them, as he was the cause of all their happiness. But the traveller shook his head and said kindly, "My time is up now and my debt is paid. Do you remember the dead man whose body you saved from those villains? You gave them all your money so that he would be able to rest in peace. I am that dead man." And without another word he vanished.

The wedding celebrations lasted a whole month and everyone in the kingdom rejoiced at the couple's happiness. Johannes and the princess loved each other dearly and soon had two beautiful children. The old king gave his throne to Johannes, who ruled wisely and well over the kingdom for many years. Meanwhile the king spent many happy days playing with his beloved grandchildren.

THE EMPEROR'S NEW CLOTHES

There once lived an emperor who loved new clothes. He enjoyed dressing up so much that he would sometimes change ten times a day. Important people visiting him would often be told,

"The emperor is in his dressing-room."

One day, a pair of tricksters arrived in the capital. They heard about the emperor and rubbed their hands. They went to see him and said they could weave marvellous cloth that had more wonderful colours and patterns than anyone had ever seen. Best of all, only clever people were able to see it. To stupid people it was invisible.

"My goodness," thought the emperor. "Not only will I have magnificent new clothes, but I shall be able to tell at once which of my ministers is not clever enough for his job! I must have some of this astonishing cloth immediately!" So he paid the tricksters very

The Emperor's New Clothes

large sums of money to begin work on their magical cloth.

The two men set up their weaving looms in the palace. They pretended to work very hard, although really they were doing nothing at all. After a while they asked for the very best silk that money could buy and the most splendid gold thread to be brought to them. They hid the silk and thread away in their bags and carried on pretending to work at the empty looms until late into the night.

After a few days the emperor could contain his excitement no longer.

"I must find out how the weavers are getting on," he said. Then he thought to himself, "I'm sure I shall see the clothes perfectly, but perhaps I should be very careful. I will send one of my ministers first, just to be on the safe side." So he sent his oldest and most important minister.

The minister went to the weavers' room. He looked, and then he stared, but he saw nothing!

"Oh, my word!" he said to himself. "This is terrible. I can't see anything there! Am I unfit for my job?" But of course he was careful not to say anything out loud.

The two tricksters invited the minister to admire the magnificent pattern and the beautiful colours of the cloth. "Have you ever seen anything so fine?" they asked him. The poor, bewildered minister gulped and replied.

"Er, no, no! It is certainly the finest I have ever seen. I shall tell the emperor at once how magnificent it is. But as the light is not very good, could you describe exactly the patterns and colours that you are making?" So the weavers told him in great detail exactly what they were pretending to make. The minister listened carefully and then repeated everything to the emperor.

Hans Christian Andersen

"The emperor is in the wardrobe"

Soon the weavers demanded more silks and thread, and again they hid them in their bags before continuing to work at the empty looms. A few days later, the emperor sent another minister to see if the cloth was finished. Like the first minister, the puzzled man stared and stared but could see nothing at all.

"Isn't this the most beautiful cloth you ever saw?" asked the tricksters, and they described the fabulous patterns which, of course, weren't really there at all.

"I'm not stupid, of course I'm not," thought the minister, "but I mustn't let anyone realise that I cannot see the cloth." So he agreed with the weavers that it was exquisite and hurried back to tell the emperor. Soon, everybody in the capital was talking about the wonderful new clothes being made for the emperor.

By now, the emperor thought it safe to see the cloth for himself. Accompanied by his ministers, he went to the weaving room. The two tricksters were still pretending to work without resting.

"If it please your majesty, come close and examine the ingenious pattern and the magnificent colours," they said, pointing to the empty looms.

"Dear, dear!" thought the emperor. "I can't see anything. This is most alarming. Can I be stupid? Am I unfit to be emperor?" So he said, "It is stupendous! The finest cloth we have ever seen. It has our most gracious approval." And he nodded his head several times as he gazed at the empty looms. The ministers all looked, but not one of them could see a thing.

"Yes, very pretty, very pretty," they all repeated, trying to look wise and serious. "You should wear the new clothes in the next procession," they advised the emperor.

The day before the procession, the two tricksters sat up all night finishing the emperor's new clothes. The townspeople could see them

Hans Christian Andersen

"Oh, how well they look! How capitally they fit!"

The Emperor's New Clothes

working in their candle-lit room. The weavers pretended to lift the cloth off the looms, cut it with large scissors and sew it with needles and thread. In the morning they announced that the clothes were finished.

When the emperor entered the room, accompanied by his ministers, each trickster held out one arm as if he was holding something.

"Here are the trousers and the waistcoat," said one.

"Here is the shirt and the coat," said the other. "They are light as cobwebs. It will feel as if you are wearing nothing at all!"

Then the emperor took off all his clothes and the tricksters pretended to dress him while he turned and twirled in front of the mirror.

"What a perfect fit!" said everyone. "What vivid colours! What beautiful clothes they are!" The emperor's servants pretended to pick up the long train and hold it in the air while the emperor stepped outside to lead the procession.

"I shall wear my new clothes in the grand procession," said the emperor. "I want all my people to see how splendidly I am dressed and what clever tailors I employ."

So the emperor mounted his horse and rode in splendour through the streets of the city while all the townspeople looked on and exclaimed, "What gorgeous new clothes! How well they fit the emperor! How perfectly they are cut!" Not one of them dared to admit that they saw nothing in case other people thought them stupid or unfit for their jobs.

Then, all of a sudden, a little boy called out, "Look! The emperor's got nothing on!"

The crowd laughed, and the little boy's father went very red.

"He's only a child," he said. "Take no notice of him. Why, he hasn't even started school yet."

But the little boy insisted, "The emperor's got nothing on," he said at the top of his voice. The crowd began to whisper among themselves.

"What did he say?" asked those who hadn't heard.

"He said the emperor's got nothing on," the others replied.

"Why, that's just what I thought," said some of the crowd. "The little boy's right."

As word spread through the crowd people began laughing and calling out, "Look! The emperor's in his birthday suit! He's got nothing on at all!"

When the emperor heard them he went very red. In his heart he knew they were right but he dared not show it.

"I must go on pretending and carry on with the procession," he thought. And his servants looked straight ahead and went on carrying the train that wasn't there!

THE HARDY TIN SOLDIER

There were once twenty-five tin soldiers, all of whom were brothers because they had been made from the same tin spoon. Each soldier rested his musket on his shoulder and stared straight ahead. They wore the same red and blue uniform, and they all looked very smart. The first words they ever heard were "Tin soldiers!" and they were cried by a little boy as he took the lid off their box. He had been given the tin soldiers for his birthday. He clapped his hands with excitement and lined the soldiers up on the table. The soldiers were identical to each other, except for one; he was the last soldier to have been made and there had not been enough tin to finish him. All the other soldiers had two legs, but he only had one. Yet it is this soldier that became the most remarkable.

On the table there were lots of other toys, but the most amazing of all was a castle made of cardboard. It had little windows looking into a great hall and in front of the castle were some trees and a round mirror that looked like a great lake. Wax swans swam on the lake, and their beautiful reflections could be seen swimming in the mirror glass. The castle was very pretty, but the prettiest part of all was a ballerina who stood at the castle door. She was made of paper and she wore a lace dress with a deep-blue ribbon over her shoulders. In the middle of the ribbon was a big tinsel rose. The ballerina had one leg lifted so high that the tin soldier could not see it, so he thought that she had one leg – just like him.

"I wish I could marry her," thought the soldier, "but she's wealthy and lives in a grand castle. I only live in a box, and there are twenty-five of us in it. She couldn't live with us, but I would like to get to know her better."

He lay down behind a match box on the table so that he could watch the ballerina, who could stand on one leg all day without losing her balance.

That evening, the soldiers were put away in their box and everyone in the house went to bed. The rest of the toys started playing and the tin soldiers rattled against the lid of the box because they wanted to play too. The nutcracker did somersaults and there was so much noise that the canary woke up and started singing. The only two who were silent were the tin soldier and the ballerina. She stood very still on her dainty pointed toes and she looked so graceful that the tin soldier never turned his eyes away from her.

The clock struck twelve and – bounce! The lid flew off the match box and out popped a goblin. It was a trick box like the kind used for playing practical jokes.

"Tin soldier," said the goblin, "don't stare at things that are none of your business!"

The Hardy Tin Soldier

But the tin soldier pretended not to hear.

"Just wait until tomorrow!" cried the goblin.

In the morning, the children woke up and the tin soldier was put on the window sill. Maybe it was the goblin, or maybe it was just a draught, but suddenly the window flew open and the tin soldier fell out. It was a terrible fall. The tin soldier landed upside down with his helmet stuck between two paving stones.

The little boy came to search for the tin soldier. He almost trod on him, but he did not even notice. The tin soldier could have shouted, "Here I am!" but he did not think it would be respectable while he was wearing his uniform.

It began to rain and the drops fell heavier and heavier until a stream formed. When it had stopped raining, two little boys came along.

"Look! A tin soldier! Let's make a boat for him!" said one of the boys.

The boys made a boat out of newspaper and put the tin soldier in it. He sailed down the gutter while the boys ran beside him clapping their hands. But the water was running very fast and the boat rocked from side to side so much that the tin soldier trembled. Yet he was a very brave soldier, so he kept his musket on his shoulder and carried on staring straight ahead.

Suddenly, the boat sailed into a drain and everything went as dark as if the soldier were in his box.

"Where am I?" he thought. "It's the goblin's fault! I wish the ballerina was here with me – it could be twice as dark and I wouldn't be scared at all if she were by my side."

All of a sudden an enormous sewer rat appeared.

"Where's your passport?" snivelled the rat.

The tin soldier stayed silent and held his musket tighter than ever. The boat sailed on, but the rat chased after it. He gnashed his teeth and ordered all the debris in the drain to block the boat's path.

"Stop him! Stop him! He hasn't paid the toll – he hasn't shown his passport!" cried the rat.

The water flowed faster and faster and at last the tin soldier could see daylight, but then he heard a roaring noise that would frighten even the bravest soldier. Where the tunnel ended, the water flowed into a great canal. Going into that would be just as dangerous as being carried over a huge waterfall.

The boat was so near to the canal that there was no way the soldier could stop it in time. He stood as straight as he could. He didn't bat an eyelid as the boat whirled round and round three or four times until it was full of water and had begun to sink. The tin soldier was up to his neck in water. The boat sank deeper and deeper until the water was over his head. He thought of the pretty ballerina and he realised that he would never see her again. In his mind he heard the words, "Farewell, farewell, you brave warrior, for today you must die!"

Then the boat broke in two and the tin soldier fell out. At that moment, he was swallowed by a giant fish.

It was even darker in the fish's body than it was in the drain tunnel, and it was also very narrow. Yet the brave tin soldier kept hold of his musket and did not move a muscle.

The fish swam and swam, making the most wonderful movements, until all at once it was still. Suddenly, a flash of light like lightning shot through it and the tin soldier was in brilliant daylight.

"The tin soldier!" cried a little boy.

The fish had been caught, carried to market and taken home to be cooked, where it had been cut open. The boy grabbed the tin soldier and carried him into a room where everyone was anxious to see this brave and remarkable soldier that had travelled around inside a fish. The tin soldier was placed on a table and by a wonderful stroke of luck he saw that it was the same room he had been in before, with the same children and the same toys. And there, stood at the castle door was his beloved ballerina, still balancing so gracefully on one leg. "She is more remarkable than I could ever be!" he thought. The tin soldier was almost weeping, but he held back his tears because he wanted the ballerina to see that he was brave. He looked at the ballerina and she looked at him, but they said nothing.

Suddenly, one of the boys grabbed the tin soldier and threw him into the fire. He had no reason for doing it; perhaps it was the goblin's work.

The tin soldier stood in the flames, burning like a brilliant light. The heat was terrible, but he could not tell whether it came from the flame of the fire or the flame in his heart. The colours of his smart uniform dripped from him as the flames licked up. He looked at the ballerina and she looked at him. He could feel himself melting, but he stood tall and kept his musket on his shoulder. Then, a sudden gust of wind caught the ballerina in its grip. She flew up into the air like a feather and landed on the fire next to the tin soldier. She flashed up in a white flame and was gone, and then the tin soldier melted down into a lump of molten tin. But the next day, when the boy's mother was clearing out the hearth, she found him in the shape of a little tin heart. Next to it was the only thing left of the ballerina; a burned tinsel rose, which was as black as coal.

WHAT THE OLD MAN DOES IS ALWAYS RIGHT

I will tell you a story which was told to me when I was a little boy. Every time I thought of the story, it seemed to get better; for this is how it goes with stories the older you become.

Imagine a house in the country, with a thatched roof, a stork's nest on the roof, low walls, a little pond with ducks and a guard dog who barks at all newcomers. There was an old man and his wife who lived in this house, with a horse that he used to go to town. His neighbours often borrowed the horse and gave some service in return. As he became older, the neighbours suggested that he sell the horse for something that might be useful to them. But *what*?

"You'll know that best, old man," said the wife. "It's nice weather today, so ride into town and get as much as you can for the horse, or exchange him for something else."

And so she fastened his scarf, brushed his hat with her hand and sent him off with a kiss and a wave. The old man rode off to sell the horse or to barter it for something else. He knew what to do.

It was a hot day without a cloud in the sky. The road was very dusty, what with all the people heading for the market. There was no shelter anywhere from the hot sunbeams.

Amongst the crowd, a man was trudging along, driving a cow to market. The cow was as beautiful a cow as the old man had ever seen, who thought to himself, "She gives good milk, I'm sure. That would be a good exchange – the horse for the cow."

"Hello there, you with the cow!" he said. "I tell you what – I reckon a horse costs more than a cow, but I'm not worried about that; a cow would be more useful to me. If you like, we'll swap?"

"To be sure, I will!" said the man, and they exchanged there and then.

That could have been the end of it and the old man could have returned home, but he decided to press on to the market. As he led his new cow along, he overtook a man with a sheep. It was a good fat sheep, with a fine fleece on its back.

"I think I'd like that sheep," said the old man to himself. "He would find plenty of grass by the cottage and in the winter we could keep him in the room with us. He would be more practical than a cow."

"Hey, you with the sheep," he said; "would you like to swap for my fine cow?"

"That would be fine," said the other man, so they exchanged there and then.

Soon, the old man was on his way again, when he overtook another man, who had a great goose under his arm. He called to him, "That's a heavy thing you have there. It has lots of feathers and plenty of fat and would look well tied to a string and paddling in the little pond at our place. My wife has so often said, 'if only we had a goose!' Perhaps you would like to exchange for this fine sheep?"

The other man was delighted to swap and so the old man continued on his way with the goose under his arm.

By this time, he was close to town. The crowd on the road had become bigger and bigger and there was a crush of men and cattle. There were so many people that they strayed into the garden of the man who kept the toll gate. In his garden was a chicken, tied up so that it wouldn't run off into the crowd.

The old man looked at the hen and decided that it was the finest he had ever seen. He thought to himself, "Why, that fowl is finer than the parson's brood hen. Upon my word, I'd like to have that chicken and I think it would be a good exchange for my goose."

He caught the eye of the toll house keeper and asked, "Shall we exchange, my good man?"

"That would be no bad thing!" replied the man.

And so they exchanged and the old man decided to stop for a drink, as he was tired after all the walking. He was about to step into the inn, when the innkeeper came out with a sack.

"What have you in your sack?" asked the old man.

"Rotten apples," replied the innkeeper. "Enough to feed the pigs for a while."

"Why, that's a terrible waste," said the old man. "Only last year, my wife was upset that our tree bore but a single apple. I should like to take your sackful of apples to show her."

What the Old Man Does is Always Right

"'I LIKE THAT!' EXCLAIMED BOTH THE ENGLISHMEN TOGETHER"

"What will you give me for them?" asked the innkeeper.

"I'll give you this fine fowl in exchange," said the old man.

And so he handed over the chicken and took the sack of rotten apples.

He walked into the inn and rested the sack beside the stove and went and found a table. But he had not realised that the stove was hot. There were many guests in the inn, including two Englishmen who were so rich that their pockets bulged with gold coins.

After a while, there came a hissing sound from the stove. The apples were beginning to roast!

"What's that noise?" demanded one of the Englishmen.

"Why, don't you know...?" said the old man. And he began to tell the whole tale of how he had swapped his horse for a cow, and all the rest of it, right down to the rotten apples.

After listening to his story, one of the Englishmen said, "Old man, your wife is going to give you a hard time when you get home! She will be furious with you!"

"Oh no, how wrong you are!" replied the old man. "She will kiss me and say, 'What the old man does is always right.'"

"Shall we bet on it, old man?" said the Englishman. "We'll wager a barrel of gold that she gives you a hard time!"

"Done!" said the old man.

With that, they took the innkeeper's carriage back to the old man's cottage.

"Good evening, dear wife," said the old man.

"Good evening, old man," she greeted him in return.

"I've made the exchange," he said.

"Well you know what you're doing," said his wife.

She took no notice of the strangers and neither did she notice the sack of rotten apples.

"I got a cow in exchange for the horse," explained the old man.

"Heaven be thanked!" she replied. "What glorious milk we shall now have, and butter and cheese on the table. That was a good exchange."

"Yes, but I swapped the cow for a sheep, then the sheep for a goose. And after that I exchanged the goose for a fowl."

"My, you're a clever man!" she said "That *was* a good exchange, for the chicken will lay eggs and soon we'll have a yard-full!"

"Yes, but then I swapped the hen for a sackful of shrivelled apples," he explained.

"What! I must kiss you for that," exclaimed his wife. "My dear husband, I asked to borrow some herbs from our neighbour this evening. She's a mean woman and said that nothing grows in her garden, not even a shrivelled apple. But now I could give her a sackful!" And with that she gave him a big hug and a huge kiss!

The two Englishmen laughed to see such joy, "I like that!" they exclaimed together. "Always going downhill and always so merry! That's got to be worth the money!"

So they paid a barrel of gold to the old peasant, who was never scolded but always kissed.

And now you see, that is my story. I heard it when I was a child and now you have heard it too!

THE STORKS

On the roof of a house, in a little village, there was a stork's nest. The mother stork sat in the nest with her four young storks, which stretched out their pointy black beaks. Nearby, the father stork stood very still and upright. He was all alone on the ridge of the roof, keeping guard over the nest. He looked very grand standing there on one leg, and he was so still that he could have been a wooden statue. "I have to look very posh so that people will think my wife is important enough to have her own security guard," he thought.

In the street below, a group of children were playing. When they saw the stork's nest one of the loudest boys started to sing an old song. The others joined in, but they could not remember all of it:

The Storks

"Stork, Stork, flay away;
Don't stand on one leg today.
Your wife is in the nest,
Where she rocks your children to rest.
The first will be hanged,
The second will be hit,
The third will be shot,
And the fourth roasted on the spit."

"Listen to what they're singing!" said the young storks. "They're saying we'll be hanged and killed!"

"Don't listen to them." said the mother stork. "Don't listen and then you won't worry."

But the boys carried on singing and mocking the storks. All except a boy called Peter, who said that it was cruel to mock animals and refused to join in.

The mother stork comforted her young. "Don't let it worry you," she said. "See how brave and still your father is standing – and he's only standing on one leg."

"But we're afraid!" said the young storks, and they cowered in the nest.

The next day, the boys returned. When they saw the storks they started to sing their song:

"The first will be hanged,
The second will be hit..."

"Will we be hanged and beaten up?" asked the young storks.

"No," replied the mother stork. "But you must learn to fly – I'll teach you. Then we shall fly out to the meadow and say hello to the frogs. When they pop up their heads and sing 'Co-ax! Co-ax,' we'll eat them up."

"And then what?" asked the young storks.

"Then all the storks in the country will gather and the autumn flying exercises will begin. You must learn to fly well or you'll die, so pay attention and try hard."

"But then we'll be killed — just as the boys say. We can hear them now."

"Listen to me and not to them," said the mother stork. "After the flying exercises, we will fly to a warm country called Egypt, which is far away over high mountains and green forests. When we get there you will see three stone houses called pyramids, which point up into the sky. They are older than you can imagine! There is a river there that floods every year and turns all the land to mud, full of delicious frogs to eat."

"Oh!" cried the young storks.

"Yes! It's wonderful! We'll spend all day eating. We'll be comfortable and happy in Egypt, but here the trees will be bare and it will be so cold that the clouds will freeze and fall down in little pieces like cotton."

The mother stork was talking about snow.

"And will the boys freeze to pieces and fall down?" asked the young storks.

"No, they won't freeze to pieces, but they will get very cold and they'll have to sit in dark rooms and cower. But you will be able to fly around in the sunshine where there are lots of wonderful flowers."

Time passed, and the young storks had grown so big that they could stand upright in the nest and look all around. Every day, the father stork brought them delicious frogs, little snakes and other stork delicacies to eat. He performed funny acts for them by laying

The Storks

THE STORKS

his head upon his tail and clapping with his beak, and then he told them stories about the marshes. "Now it's time to learn to fly," said the mother stork one day. So the four young storks went out onto the ridge of the nest. They tried to balance with their wings, but they kept falling over.

"Watch me," said the mother stork. "You have to hold your heads like this, and put your feet like this. One, two! One, two! That will help."

Then the mother stork flew a few metres and the young storks leapt clumsily. But they fell down because their bodies were too heavy.

"I will not fly!" said one of the young storks, and he crept back to the nest. "I don't care about going to Egypt!"

"Do you want to freeze to death here when the winter arrives? Do you want the boys to sing at you, and then shoot you and roast you for dinner? I'll call them for you."

"No!" cried the young stork. He hopped back on to the roof and joined the others.

By the third day of practising the storks could fly a little, but they also thought they could soar and hover in the air. They tried but they tumbled down and had to flap their wings as quick as they could. The boys in the street came and sang their song:

"Stork, stork, flay away!"

"Shall we fly down and peck them?" asked the young storks.

"No," replied the mother stork, "leave them alone and listen to me, what I'm saying is far more important. One, two, three! Fly to the right! One, two, three! Fly to the left, round the chimney. Well done. The last kick you did with your feet was very good. You will be allowed to fly to the marsh with me tomorrow. Lots of nice

The Storks

stork families go there with their young storks, and I want to show them that mine are the nicest and the best fliers."

"But can't we get our own back on those boys?" asked the young storks.

"Let them scream as much as they like. You will fly up into the clouds and go to the land of the pyramids, while they'll have to shiver and there won't be a single green leaf or juicy apple around."

"Shhhh – we'll get our revenge ourselves!" the young storks whispered to one other, and then they continued practising.

The boy singing loudest was the one who had started the song in the first place. He was only six years old and he was very little. But the young storks thought that he must be a hundred, because he was so much bigger than their mother or father. It was this boy that they wanted to get their revenge upon. The young storks were very angry, and as they got bigger they were less patient. Finally, their mother agreed that they would get their revenge, but not until the day before they were due to leave for Egypt.

"First, we have to see how well you behave at the marsh," said the mother stork. "If you don't fly well, the chief stork will peck you with his beak and you won't be allowed to come with us to Egypt. Then the boy will be right and you'll end up on the spit."

"We'll fly the very best we can!" cried the young storks, and they practised hard every day until they could fly so well that they looked neat and graceful.

Soon, it was autumn and all the storks were preparing for the long journey to Egypt. But the young ones had to pass their flying test first. They flew over forests and villages to show how well they could soar. The young storks did incredibly well and got the highest mark possible: "Remarkably well, with frogs and snakes on top!"

And as an extra reward they were even allowed to eat the frogs and snakes.

"Now we'll get our revenge!" they said.

"Yes, we will!" said the mother stork. "I've thought of a good way to pay that cruel little boy back. I know a pond where all the human babies sleep before a stork takes them to their parents. They lie there dreaming sweetly all day long. When the parents receive their baby they are overjoyed, and all the little boys and girls are delighted to have a little brother or sister. We'll fly to the pond and each take a little brother or sister to all the girls and boys in the village, except to the boys who sang and mocked us."

"But what about the meanest boy? The one who started the song!" screamed the young storks.

"We'll take him a brother or sister that has dreamed itself into eternal sleep. Then he'll be sad because he'll have no one to play with. But do you remember that good little boy named Peter? He refused to join in with the singing so we'll take him a brother and a sister this year. Peter was such a good boy that I'm going to name you all Peter too."

So all the young storks were named Peter, and after delivering the babies they set off for Egypt.

THE UGLY DUCKLING

It was a glorious summer, with yellow cornfields and hay stacked up neatly in the green meadows. The stork went about on his long, red legs chattering in Egyptian, for this was the language he had learned from his mother. All around the fields and meadows were great forests and in the midst of these were deep lakes.

The fields belonged to a lovely old farm, which was surrounded by lazy canals with wildlife all around. In the canal beside the old barn, there was a duck sitting upon her nest, waiting for her eggs to hatch.

At last, one eggshell after another burst open. "Piep! Piep!" each duckling cried, as its head popped out of the shell. In a while, they were all free of their shells and were excited to see the green leaves and blue water all around them.

The Ugly Duckling

"How wide the world is!" said the young ducklings. For they certainly had more room now they were free from their eggs.

"Do you think that this is all the world?" asked their mother. "That extends beyond the garden over there and into the meadow," she said, "though I've not been there myself." She wiggled a bit and stood up to lead her new brood, but noticed that one egg had yet to hatch. It was the biggest of them all. "I hope this one is as pretty as you all!" she exclaimed.

An old drake came along and said, "That's not a duck's egg! It's a turkey egg!"

The mother duck was most put out and replied, "I think not! It's just a very large duckling! I'll sit here a while longer until it hatches."

At last the great egg burst. "Piep! Piep!" it went and out popped the occupant of the shell. It was very large and very ugly! The duck looked at it.

"It's a very large duckling!" she said, "none of the others look like that. Can it really be a turkey chick? Now we shall soon find out, for it's coming for a swim tomorrow, like it or not!"

The weather was beautiful the next day and the sun shone through the trees. The mother duck went down to the water with her new brood behind her. With a splash, she jumped in and they all followed behind her. The ugly, grey duckling swam with the rest. The mother duck was delighted and exclaimed, "See how it swims! It's my own child and not so ugly if you catch it in the right light! Quack, quack, come with me and I'll lead you out into the poultry yard and then the wide world."

They soon came upon the poultry yard, where two families of ducks were squabbling over a bit of fish. The cat took it in the end and the argument was settled.

"Come along children!" demanded the mother duck. "Let's show the world our best appearance. Come now, shake your tails and don't turn in your toes! A well-brought-up duck points its toes and bends its neck nicely!"

The grand-looking Spanish duck and all the other ducks in the yard watched the mother duck and her brood waddle by.

They weren't impressed by the newcomers and especially by the ugly grey one. One nasty duck flew up and bit it on the neck!

"Leave it alone!" screamed the mother duck. "It's done no harm to you!"

"Yes, but it's too large and weird looking," said the nasty duck.

"It's very peculiar," said the Spanish duck, "they're all very pretty except that one. I wish we could alter its appearance!"

"Well, that can't be done, Madam," declared the mother duck, with much irritation. "It swims well and will become smaller and better looking in time. What's more, it is a drake and will be very strong and do well in the world."

"Hmm, we'll see!" said the Spanish duck. "Make yourselves at home, but make sure you find something tasty for me to eat."

But the poor ugly duckling was soon set upon one by one by all the other ducks and birds in the yard. "It is too big!" they all exclaimed. The turkey cock, who was the toughest of them all, puffed up his feathers to make himself look enormous and raced around the ugly duckling until he became red in the face.

So it went on, day after day. The poor ugly duckling was bullied and beaten by everyone, even his brothers and sisters, who said, "If only the cat would catch you and put an end to it all!"

Even the girl who fed the poultry kicked at it with her foot. The ugly ducking became so upset that it shut its eyes and took flight over the yard fence and into the woods beyond the meadow. By nightfall, it came upon a lake shore, where it landed and lay down all night. Towards morning the wild ducks found the ugly duckling amongst them. They gathered round and said, "And who are you? You are remarkably ugly! It does not matter to us so long as you don't marry one of our family."

Poor thing, all it could think of was to find some water and a little to eat! Here it stayed for two whole days, then two wild geese crept up beside him. Like him, they were not long out of their eggs.

"Listen pal," said one of them. "You're so ugly that I like you! Will you come with us out onto the wild moor and meet the other geese? You have a chance of making your fortune, even though you're so ugly."

With that, there was a loud "bang, bang" and the two geese fell down dead as a whole flock of birds took off into the sky. What a fright! The hunters' dogs came racing through the shallows and came right up to the ugly duckling's beak. They sniffed and growled and ran on to their masters.

"Oh, heavens," said the ugly duckling. "I am so ugly that even the dogs don't want to bite me!"

The poor thing hid in the reeds all day long, while the hunt went on around him. Eventually, the guns fell silent and it began to rain, first a few drops and then a torrential gale. The ugly duckling made his way to a little hut, where there was a gap in the broken old door. He squeezed through the gap and inside he found an old woman, with her cat called Tom and a brown hen. The cat began to purr and the hen to cluck, so that the old woman noticed the duckling at her feet.

"What's this?" said the old woman. But she could not see well and thought that the cat had brought in a fat duck that had strayed.

"My, this is a grand prize. Soon we shall have duck eggs!"

And so the duck was allowed to stay in the old hut, but no eggs came. The hen and the cat were not impressed and wanted to make sure that the ugly duckling didn't mess up their comfortable lives.

"Can you lay eggs?" enquired the hen.

"No," said the duckling.

"Then you'll have the goodness not to argue with me!" said the hen.

"Can you arch your back and spit and purr whenever you like?" asked the cat.

"No," said the duckling.

"Then you cannot have any opinion of your own!" said the cat.

So the ugly duckling sat in a corner, with only his dreams of paddling in the water to comfort him. After a few days, he decided to go away and leave the hut and with it the miserable cat and hen.

He flew off and soon found some water. But he was shunned by every creature that came upon him because of his ugliness.

Soon it became autumn and the leaves in the forest turned yellow and brown and were gone. The wind blew up and it became colder and colder. Then one day, the ugly duckling saw a whole flock of the most handsome and beautiful white birds he had ever seen. They had dazzlingly long necks and a strange cry. The birds lined up to take off down the water and circled around the lake so that the ugly duckling had to turn round and round to watch them. He bobbed up and down in the water and they were gone! He felt a terrible aching in his heart as they vanished into the sky and could only think of possessing the loveliness of the birds whose name he did not know.

The Ugly Duckling

"The new one is the most beautiful of all"

The winter came and it became colder and colder. The ugly duckling was forced to swim around in the water to stop the surface from freezing. But every night the hole in which he swam became smaller and smaller. The duck had to paddle and paddle to stop the hole from freezing over, but he became exhausted and soon he was stuck fast in the ice.

Early in the morning, a peasant came by and saw what had happened. He took his wooden shoe and broke the ice and carried the duckling home to his wife and children. The children were excited and wanted to play with the duckling, but the duckling was frightened and in its terror managed to knock over the milk pan and he flew into the butter tub! He struggled out and took off again, heading for the open door and freedom beyond.

The tale would be sadder still if I told you of all the misery that the ugly duckling had to endure all winter long, on the freezing cold moor amongst all the unfriendly creatures.

Then one day the larks began to sing and the sun came up. It was a beautiful spring and all of a sudden the duckling could fly better than ever before. It found itself in a great garden, where the elder-trees smelled sweet as they bent their branches down to the canal that wound through the garden. And there from a thicket came three of the beautiful white birds that he had seen, gently gliding along the water.

The ugly duckling decided that he would fly amongst them and be killed by these royal birds – better than to be pursued and beaten by ducks and chickens and little girls in the poultry yard. He flew out into their midst and cried, "Kill me!" The poor creature expected nothing but death, but what was this in the glassy water's surface? He beheld his own image and lo! No longer was he an ugly, grey duckling, but a beautiful and graceful swan!

The Ugly Duckling

The great swans swam around him and stroked him and for the first time he felt loved and happy.

Into the garden came little children, who threw bread and corn into the water. The youngest of them cried, "There is a new one! Look, a beautiful new swan!"

The parents and children clapped their hands and danced with excitement to see the latest arrival. The new swan felt quite ashamed, for he did not know what to do. He was so happy, yet not at all proud. He thought how he had been persecuted and despised and now he heard them saying that he was the most beautiful of all the birds. Then his wings rustled and he lifted his long neck and cried with rejoice from the depths of his heart, "I never dreamed of so much happiness when I was the ugly duckling!"

THE SHEPHERDESS AND THE CHIMNEY-SWEEPER

There was once a very old wooden cupboard, darkened with age and decorated with carved foliage and patterns. It had been handed down from a great-grandmother, and it was covered with carved roses and tulips. There were stags with large antlers and a man had been carved into the middle of the cupboard door. He looked very funny: he had a big grin, legs like a goat, little horns on his head and a long beard. The children of the house called him Mr Billygoat-Legs-Lieutenant-and-Major-General-War-Commander-Sergeant. He looked at the table under the mirror, on which stood a little shepherdess made of china. She wore a gold hat and shoes, and she held a shepherd's crook. Her dress had a big red rose on it and she looked very pretty. Next to her there stood a chimney-sweeper. He was painted black, but because he didn't actually sweep any chimneys he was clean and neat. The factory that made him could have just as easily painted him to look like a prince.

The chimney-sweeper and the shepherdess had been standing next to each other for so long that they had become engaged. They suited each other well because they were both made of the same brittle china.

Near to them there stood a man that was three times their size. He was also made of porcelain and had been made so skilfully that he could nod his head. He claimed that he was the grandfather of the shepherdess and that she must do what he said. He had agreed to let Mr Billygoat-Legs-Lieutenant-and-Major-General-War-Commander-Sergeant marry her.

"You will marry him!" said the nodding man. "He is carved of the finest mahogany and he has a whole cupboard full of silver plates."

"I refuse to go to that dark cupboard!" said the shepherdess. "I've heard that he has eleven porcelain wives in there already!"

"Then you will be the twelfth!" cried the nodding man. "Tonight, as soon as the old cupboard starts to rattle, you will be married."

With that, he nodded his head and fell asleep. The little shepherdess wept and looked at her beloved chimney-sweeper.

"We can't stay here!" she cried. "Run away with me to the wide world outside!"

"I'll do whatever you want," replied the chimney-sweeper. "Let's start right away. I can earn enough to support us by sweeping chimneys."

"But first we need to get down from the table," she said. "I won't be happy until we're out in the wide world."

The chimney-sweeper showed her how to get down from the table by using the carved corners and foliage as steps. He also got his ladder to help her, and soon they were on the floor. But when they looked up at the cupboard they saw that there was a great commotion. All the carved stags were stretching their heads out and rearing up their antlers. Mr Billygoat-Legs-Lieutenant-and-Major-General-War-Commander-Sergeant leapt into the air and called to the nodding man, "They're running away! They're running away!"

The chimney-sweeper and the shepherdess were so frightened that they jumped into a drawer. Inside, there were three or four incomplete packs of cards and a puppet show theatre where they staged plays. All the ladies, diamonds, clubs, hearts and spades sat in the first row fanning themselves while the jacks stood behind them. The play was about two people who wanted to marry each other, but were not allowed to. The shepherdess wept because it was just like her and the chimney-sweeper.

"I can't bear it," she said. "I have to go outside."

They jumped back down onto the floor. But when they looked up they saw that the nodding man was awake – and he was shaking with rage.

"The nodding man is coming!" cried the little shepherdess, and she was so startled that she fell over.

"I have an idea," said the chimney-sweeper. "Why don't we sneak into the potpourri vase? Then we can lie on a bed of roses and lavender, and we'll throw salt at the nodding man if he comes anywhere near us."

"That won't help," she replied. "The nodding man and the potpourri vase used to be engaged and I know she still loves him. We'll have to go out into the wide world."

"Are you really brave enough to go out into the wide world with me?" asked the chimney-sweeper. "Have you thought about how wide it is, and how we can never come back once we've gone?"

"I have," she replied.

The chimney-sweeper looked at her fondly and said, "Let's go up through the chimney. We'll creep into the stove, walk through the iron box and crawl along the pipe. Then we can climb up the chimney, so high that they'll never catch us. At the top there's a hole that leads to the wide world."

"It looks very dark in there," she said. But she went with him into the dark stove, through the iron box and along the pipe.

"Now we're in the chimney," he said. "Look, you can see the beautiful stars shining in the sky."

A glittering star shone down on them as if to light the way. They clambered up the chimney. It was very steep, but the chimney-sweeper held the shepherdess and helped her by showing her the best places to rest her porcelain feet. At last, they reached the edge of the chimney. They were extremely tired so they sat and rested for a while.

All the stars in the night sky shone above them, and they could see all the roofs of the town below. They looked far around them at the world. But the poor shepherdess had not realised that the world would be this wide. She leant against the chimney-sweeper and wept so hard that the gold ran off her skirt.

"It's too wide!" she cried. "I can't bear it! I wish I was back on the table. I'll never be happy until I'm back there. You've brought me out into the wide world and if you really love me you'll take me home again."

The chimney-sweeper reminded her about the nodding man and Mr Billygoat-Legs-Lieutenant-and-Major-General-War-Commander-Sergeant, but the shepherdess wept and kissed him until he gave in, even though it was not a good idea.

The Shepherdess and the Chimney-Sweeper

"'HAVE YOU REALLY COURAGE TO GO INTO THE WIDE WORLD WITH ME?' ASKED THE CHIMNEY-SWEEPER"

So they climbed back down the chimney, crawled along the pipe and walked through the iron box until finally they stood in the dark stove. They stopped to listen to what was happening in the room. It was very quiet and when they looked through the stove door they saw why; the nodding man lay broken into three pieces on the floor and his head had rolled all the way into the corner of the room. He must have fallen from the table. Mr Billygoat-Legs-Lieutenant-and-Major-General-War-Commander-Sergeant was looking down at him.

"How terrible!" said the little shepherdess. "My grandfather has broken into three pieces and it's our fault! I'll never forgive myself!" She wrung her hands with worry.

"Don't worry – he can be fixed," said the chimney-sweeper. "If they glue him back together and put a rivet in his neck he'll be as good as new. He'll be back to being cruel to us in no time."

"Do you really think so?" she cried, hopefully.

They climbed back onto the table where they used to stand.

"I can't believe we're back here," said the chimney-sweeper. "We might as well just have stayed here all along."

But the shepherdess was not listening to him. "If only my grandfather were fixed," she said. "Is it expensive?"

It was not expensive and soon the nodding man was fixed. The family glued him back together and put a large rivet in his neck. He was as good as new, except that he could no longer nod.

"Ever since you broke into pieces you seem to have become too proud to let me marry the shepherdess," said Mr Billygoat-Legs-Lieutenant-and-Major-General-War-Commander-Sergeant one day. "I don't think you have any reason to look down on someone as fine and wealthy as me! Am I allowed to marry her or not?"

The Shepherdess and the Chimney-Sweeper

The shepherdess and the chimney-sweeper looked desperately at the nodding man, fearing that he would nod. But, try as he might, the nodding man could not move his head and he was too embarrassed to say anything. So the porcelain shepherdess and chimney-sweeper stayed together and loved each other until they broke.

THE FIR TREE

There was once a pretty little fir tree growing in a clearing in the middle of a forest. The warm sun shone down on it and fresh mountain breezes blew softly through its branches. The bigger trees stood around it and when the children came to gather wild berries they always sat nearby, saying, "What a sweet little fir tree!"

But the little fir tree took no notice of all this attention as he was in such a great hurry to grow bigger.

"How I wish I was as tall as the other trees!" it sighed. "The birds would build nests in my branches and I could see out over the whole world."

In winter the hares and rabbits jumped over the little tree, which made it feel even smaller. But each year it grew a little bit more until one winter it had grown so tall that the hares and rabbits had to run around it.

The Fir Tree

"Growing up to be big and tall is all that matters in this world," thought the little tree.

Every autumn the woodcutters came and chopped down the tallest trees. They fell with a terrible crash that made the little fir tree shudder. When their branches had been cut off, the trees were loaded onto carts and hauled away.

In spring, when the swallows and storks returned to the forest, the little fir tree would ask them, "Do you know what happened to the big trees? Have you seen them?"

"I think I did," said a stork. "As I flew here from Egypt, I met some new ships with shining wooden masts. I am sure they were your friends."

"Just wait until I'm big and tall enough to cross the sea!" said the little fir tree.

"Don't hurry to grow. Enjoy your youth while it lasts," the sunbeams whispered softly. The breezes kissed the tree and the dew fell like tears on its branches.

As Christmas drew near, the woodcutters felled some of the younger trees and took them away in a cart. This made the little fir tree more restless than ever.

"Where can they be going?" he said to himself. "Those trees are smaller than me. And why have their branches not been cut off?"

"We know!" twittered the sparrows. "We have peeped in through the windows in the town and seen the trees dressed up with golden apples and coloured sweets. Hundreds of candles light up their branches and they look very beautiful."

"Oh, I wonder if I will be honoured like that!" exclaimed the fir tree. "And I wonder what happens next? There must be even bigger honours to follow!"

"Enjoy what we bring," whispered the breezes and the sunbeams. "Enjoy your bright young days." But the tree would not enjoy itself and only wanted to grow.

One Christmas, the woodcutters came and cut down the fir tree, saying that it was the most beautiful in the forest. When the axe cut into its trunk, the tree fell with a groan and felt a sudden pang of sadness at leaving its familiar forest home.

It bumped along in the cart with the other trees on the journey to the town. At last they were unpacked in a courtyard and as the fir tree leaned against a wall it heard a voice say, "That one is a beauty. We'll take it."

Two servants carried the fir tree into a large, comfortable room. There was a rocking-horse standing on the polished floor, picture-books lying on the tables and toys on the shelves. The tree shook with fear as it was placed in a barrel of sand standing on a beautiful carpet.

Servants and rich young ladies began to decorate the tree. From the branches they hung coloured sweets, golden apples, walnuts and little toys. A hundred red, white and blue candles were clipped to the branches and dolls were placed under the tree. Then a sparkling golden star was placed right on top.

"If only evening would come, so the candles can be lit!" thought the tree impatiently. "Then perhaps the other trees from the forest will come and admire me, and the sparrows will peep through the window. Perhaps I will take root here and stay like this for ever! How fine!"

At last, evening came and the candles were lit. The tree looked beautiful but it was so anxious not to drop any of its ornaments that it trembled and one of the branches caught fire. After the flame was put out, the frightened tree tried hard not to shake.

Suddenly the doors flew open and a troop of children rushed into the room towards the tree. They shrieked with delight and danced around it.

The Fir Tree

"What will happen next?" thought the tree.

As each candle burned down, it was put out, and when the last little flame had gone, each child took a present. The tree was shaken and grabbed and its branches cracked painfully! The children danced around with their toys and sweets.

"A story! We want a story!" they cried, dragging a kind-looking man to a chair by the tree. He sat down, saying, "Perhaps the tree would like to hear the story too. What shall it be? Cinderella or Humpty-Dumpty?"

"Cinderella!" some cried. "Humpty-Dumpty!" cried the others. Their squabbling voices filled the air and only the fir tree was silent, "Don't I have a say?" he thought. "After all, I am part of this evening too."

In the end, the man told the story of Humpty-Dumpty who, although he fell down the stairs, still won great honours and married a princess.

"Humpty-Dumpty fell down the stairs but still married a princess! Of course, that is what happens in the wide world," said the fir tree, who thought it was a true story. "So, if I fell down the stairs I might get a princess too." The tree felt happy at the thought that next day he would be decorated again with toys, candles and sweets. "Tomorrow, I will not tremble," he thought. "Tomorrow, I will enjoy my great honour and hear the story of Humpty-Dumpty again."

Next morning, when the servants came in, the tree thought, "Now I'm going to be dressed in my finery again." But instead they dragged him upstairs and flung him on the floor in a dark corner. "What am I doing here?" thought the unhappy tree. And he lay there wondering, waiting for someone to come.

The days passed and the wintry weather got colder.

"The ground is too hard for them to plant me," thought the little tree. "I'm being kept indoors until spring. How kind people are! But I do wish it wasn't so cold and dark and lonely in here."

Suddenly, two little mice crept up and sniffed at the fir tree.

"Where do you come from, old fir tree?" asked one.

"Tell us what you have seen in the world – that is, if you've been there."

"Old! I'm not old!" said the fir tree, and he told the little mice all about the forest, where the warm sun shines, the soft breezes blow and the birds sing.

"You must have been very happy there, old fir tree!" squeaked the mice.

"Stop calling me old," said the fir tree indignantly. "I am not old. I only came from the forest this winter." Then it told them all about Christmas Eve and the thrill of being dressed with candles and golden apples.

The next night, the mice came again with four more mice asking the tree to tell the same story. Each time it was told, the more clearly the tree remembered everything and sighed, "Such good times will never come again but if Humpty-Dumpty can fall down the stairs and still marry a princess, perhaps I will meet a princess one day."

"Tell us about Humpty-Dumpty!" cried the mice. So the fir tree told the story and the little mice squeaked and jumped with excitement. Next night, more mice came, and on Sunday two rats joined the crowd as well.

"Is that the only story you know?" asked one rat.

"Only that one," said the tree. "I heard it on the happiest evening of my life, although I didn't know that at the time."

"Pah! It's a stupid story," said the rat. "Don't you know anything about cheese or store-cupboards?"

The Fir Tree

"No. I'm sorry, I don't," replied the tree. The mice and rats left, and the tree lay in the cold and dark with only memories for comfort.

One day, the servants came and dragged the tree outside.

"Now I begin my new life," it thought as it felt the fresh air and warm sunshine. The servants carried the tree into a garden where sweet-smelling roses grew over the walls, trees were in blossom and swallows darted through the air.

"I shall live happily here!" thought the tree, spreading out its yellow, withered branches. But the servants threw the tree into the nettles and weeds and two little children ran up and jumped on the branches until they cracked.

"Look what I've found sticking to the ugly old fir tree," said one, and tore off the golden star that had once sparkled and shone so brightly.

The tree looked at the beautiful garden and remembered its life in the forest, the happy Christmas Eve and the little mice who loved to hear the story of Humpty-Dumpty.

"It's all over," said the old tree. "If only I had realised true happiness when I had it."

A servant chopped the fir tree into pieces and carried them into the kitchen. The wood burned fast and the tree's sighs sounded like gun-shots. The tree was dreaming of a summer's day or a winter's night in the forest, of Christmas and of Humpty-Dumpty, the only story he knew. The children came to sit near the fire. The youngest boy clutched the golden star as he gazed into the flames. At last, there was nothing left but a heap of ashes.

THE SWINEHERD

There was once a poor prince who ruled a small kingdom. One day, he decided to find himself a wife. There were lots of princesses all over the land who would have been delighted to marry the handsome prince, but he decided to ask the emperor's daughter.

The prince's father had died many years before, and on his grave grew a very beautiful rose bush. It only bloomed once every five years, and even then it only produced a single rose. It was the most incredible rose in the land. It was so sweet that anyone who smelt it forgot all their sorrows and worry. The prince also had a nightingale, which could sing all the songs in the world. He decided to give the rosebush and the nightingale to the princess, and so he put them into big silver boxes and sent them to her.

The emperor demanded that the presents be brought to him in the great hall. The princess was there with her maids and when she saw the presents she clapped her hands with joy.

The Swineherd

"I hope it's a little kitten!" she said.

But then out came the rosebush with the beautiful rose.

"It's so pretty and very well made!" said the court ladies.

"It's more than pretty," said the emperor, "it is wonderful."

But when the princess touched the rose she began to cry.

"Father," she said, "it's not artificial, it's a *natural* rose! I don't like *natural* things!"

"Let's wait until we've seen what's in the other box before we get angry," said the emperor. Then the nightingale came out and sang so beautifully that for a few moments everyone was speechless.

"Wonderful!" said the maids.

"The bird reminds me of the late emperor's music box," said an old courtier. "It has the same tone and the same expression."

"Yes," said the emperor and then he wept like a child as he remembered his dead father.

"I hope it's not a *natural* bird!" said the princess.

"It is a *natural* bird," said the messengers who had brought the presents.

"Then let it fly away," said the princess, and she wouldn't even let the prince come to see her.

But the prince was not disheartened. He disguised himself and knocked on the castle door.

"Good day, Emperor," he said. "Have you got any jobs in the castle?"

"Yes," replied the emperor, "we need someone who can look after the pigs, because we have so many."

So the prince was appointed the palace's swineherd. He was given a tiny room next to the pigsty and all day long he sat and worked while he watched the pigs. By the evening he had finished making a little pot,

Hans Christian Andersen

"On the grave of the prince's father there grew a rose bush"

The Swineherd

which was covered in tiny bells. When the pot was boiled the bells rang and played an old song:

"*Oh, my darling Augustine,*

All is lost, all is lost."

Even better than that, when the prince dipped his finger in the smoke that came from the pot he could smell what everyone was cooking.

One day, the princess was walking past with her maids. When she heard the song she stopped and looked very pleased. She could play "*Oh, my darling Augustine*" on the piano, although it was the only song she knew.

"That's the song I play!" she cried. "He must be a very well-educated swineherd! Maid, go and ask the price of that instrument."

So one of the maids went and asked the swineherd.

"How much do you want for the pot?" asked the maid.

"I want ten kisses from the princess," replied the swineherd.

"Heaven save us!" exclaimed the maid.

"Maid, what did he say?" asked the princess.

"I don't want to repeat it," replied the maid.

"Well, whisper it in my ear." So the lady whispered it to her. "How rude!" declared the princess, and she turned and walked away. But after a few steps she heard the bells again:

"*Oh, my darling Augustine,*

All is lost, all is lost."

"Ask him if he will take ten kisses from my maids," cried the princess.

"Ten kisses from the princess, or I will keep my pot," replied the swineherd.

"How annoying!" cried the princess. "Only if my maids will stand around me so that no one can see."

So the maids stood around the princess and spread out their dresses so that no one could see her. The princess kissed the swineherd ten times and he gave her the pot.

The princess was overjoyed. All evening and all the next day the pot was kept boiling and the princess knew what every house in the town was cooking. The ladies of the court danced with joy and clapped their hands.

"We know who has soup and pancakes for dinner, and who has a quick dinner of pork cutlets; how interesting!"

"That is interesting!" agreed the head maid.

The swineherd made something new every day. One day, he made a special rattle. When it was swung, it could play every song written since the beginning of time.

"That's wonderful!" cried the princess as she walked past one day. "That's the best song I've ever heard. Go and ask the swineherd what the instrument does, but tell him I won't give him any more kisses."

So the maid asked the swineherd.

"He wants a hundred more kisses," she told the princess when she returned.

"He's mad!" exclaimed the princess, and she walked away. But after a few steps she stopped. "I must encourage the arts," she thought. "I am the emperor's daughter, after all!"

"Tell him I'll give him ten kisses, like last time, and he can have the rest from my maids," said the princess.

"We don't want to kiss the swineherd!" cried the maids.

"Don't be silly. If I can kiss him, you can. Don't forget that I put a roof over your heads and pay you all well."

So the maids asked the swineherd again.

"A hundred kisses from the princess," he said, "or I'll keep the rattle."

The Swineherd

"Fine," said the princess, "but only if my maids stand around me so that no one can see." So the maids gathered round while she kissed the swineherd.

"What is that crowd down by the pigsty?" asked the emperor as he looked out of the window. He stepped out onto his balcony, rubbed his eyes and put on his glasses. "What are the maids doing playing games when they should be watching the princess? I'll have to go down and talk to them."

The emperor hurried down to the pigsty. When he got near he crept up close to the maids so they would not hear him coming. The maids were too busy counting the kisses to notice the emperor. The emperor stood on tiptoes.

"What's that?" he cried when he saw that the princess was kissing the swineherd. He hit them both on the head with his slipper as they were about to reach the sixty-eighth kiss.

"Be gone!" he cried. He was very angry!

The princess and the swineherd were banished from the castle. The princess stood and cried, and then it started to rain.

"Oh, poor me!" cried the princess. "If only I had married the handsome prince this would never have happened! I'm so miserable!"

The swineherd hid behind a tree and took off his disguise. Then he stepped out dressed in his princely robes. He looked so handsome that the princess bowed before him.

"You are a foolish girl," he said. "You wouldn't marry me, even though I am an honest prince. You didn't value the beautiful rose or the splendid nightingale, but for a silly toy you kissed the swineherd. You have got what you deserve."

Then the prince returned to his kingdom and shut his castle door, and the princess was left standing alone outside singing:

> "Oh, my darling Augustine,
> All is lost, all is lost."

THE SNOW QUEEN

There was once a magic mirror made by an evil goblin that made everything you saw in it look the other way round. If it was a good thing you saw, it seemed bad and ugly; but if it was nasty it looked good and cheerful. Everyone who visited the school he kept declared that a wonderful thing had been made. One day it shattered into millions of tiny pieces that flew into the air and were scattered hither and thither. If one of the slivers blew into someone's eye it stuck there, making everything look horrid. Worse still, if it got into the heart it made everything cold and unpleasant.

A little girl called Gerda and a little boy called Kay lived next door to each other. They were inseparable friends and played together every day. In summer they played in the garden under the roses that hung down from the window boxes. In winter, they played indoors, listening to the stories Kay's grandmother told, or peering through the frosty windows and watching the snowflakes swirling around.

"The snowflakes are like white bees," said grandmother. "The queen bee flies in the middle of the swarm, and at night she peeps in at the windows and covers them with frozen flowers."

At bedtime that evening, Kay was peering through the window to watch the snow when one big flake landed on the edge of a flower box. It seemed to grow bigger and bigger, slowly changing into a beautiful, ice-white woman. She wore robes that seemed to be made of millions of icy stars and her eyes glittered. She smiled and waved at Kay. Behind her flew big white birds, but he was frightened and drew the curtains.

By the time summer returned, Kay had forgotten about the strange ice-woman. He and Gerda once more spent the long, warm days playing together under the roses. One day Gerda made up a little song and sang it to Kay:

"The roses bloom for just one hour, then die;

but go on living evermore, on high!"

The two children were humming the song together and looking up at the bright sky when suddenly Kay cried out, "Ow! Something has flown into my eye! Something is stinging my heart!" How could he know that these were tiny slivers of glass from the shattered magic mirror that had stuck in his eye and in his heart? Gerda tried to help but he shouted at her, "You look ugly!" and kicked the flowers saying, "Look at the wormhole in that rose, and at that twisted one! What nasty flowers!"

Then he pulled off two rose-heads and ran away. He couldn't help himself. It was the glass in his eye and his heart that made him behave like this. Winter returned, and one day he and Gerda found a magnifying-glass and looked at snowflakes through it. Kay was entranced by their perfect shapes and thought they were prettier than any flower. He took his sledge and went out to play with the boys in the town square. They were tying their sledges to passing carts to be

Hans Christian Andersen

"Those who visited the goblin school declared everywhere that a wonder had been wrought"

pulled along, so when Kay saw a big white sleigh passing slowly he tied his sledge behind it. Soon he was having great fun sliding along the snowy streets. But the big white sleigh went faster and faster and didn't stop. On and on it drove, out through the town gate and into the countryside. The sleigh-driver turned and looked at him and the cold look made Kay sit still.

It began to snow harder and harder, yet still the sleigh sped onwards. The snowflakes grew so large they looked like the big white birds Kay had seen that night through his window. He screamed at the top of his voice and tried to untie his sledge, but nobody heard him. He was so frightened that he tried to say his prayers but all he could remember were his multiplication tables from school.

Suddenly the great white sleigh stopped and the driver stepped down. Kay recognised the dazzling whiteness of the tall and slender lady he had seen through his window. It was the Snow Queen.

"If you don't wish to freeze, dear Kay, come under my bear-skin," she said. She wrapped the skin round him and it was like sinking into a snow-drift. When she kissed his forehead it seemed like a dagger in his half-frozen heart, but he was no longer cold. She kissed him again and all memory of Gerda and his grandmother vanished.

"No more kisses," said the Snow Queen, "or I shall kiss you to death."

They flew high above the black storm clouds, over forests and lakes, across the sea and foreign lands. Below them the cold wind blew, wolves howled, and black, cawing crows hovered. Above them shone the bright, clear moon.

When Kay didn't return, Gerda cried bitterly. People thought he had fallen through the ice on the river and drowned. One spring morning Gerda put on her new red shoes and set off to find him.

"Give Kay back and you can have my new red shoes," she said to the river. She threw them into the water, but they floated back to the bank. Gerda climbed into a little boat and threw them further, and the boat began to float away. The sparrows followed, singing, "Here we are!" and the red shoes bobbed along behind. "Perhaps the river will carry me to Kay," thought Gerda.

A very old woman came and said, "How did you manage to come on the great rolling river?" As she helped Gerda out of the boat she said, "Tell me who you are and how you got here?"

Gerda told her story and asked if the old woman had seen Kay, but she shook her head. Inside, the coloured windows made a strange rainbow of light in the room. The old woman gave Gerda a bowl of delicious ripe cherries to eat and combed her hair with a golden comb, which made her forget all about Kay.

"I have always longed for a little girl to come and live with me," said the old woman.

The old woman was a witch, but a kind one, and let Gerda play in her pretty garden. That night, Gerda slept on soft, silk pillows stuffed with violets, which gave her wonderful dreams. The old woman had used her magic to remove all the roses from her garden in case they reminded Gerda of Kay, but she forgot to take a rose from her hat. Gerda noticed it.

"Why are there no roses in the garden?" she said, and began to cry. Her tears fell on a buried rose-tree that sprang to life and brought memories of Kay flooding back.

"Is Kay dead?" Gerda asked the rose-tree.

"No, I haven't seen him underground," it replied.

Gerda went to the other flowers and asked them, "Do you know where Kay is?" But instead of answering, each flower told a

The Snow Queen

"How do you manage to come on the great rolling river?"

different story. At last, Gerda was tired of listening to them and ran to the big, wooden gate. She ran barefoot into the wide world.

"I've stayed too long!" she said, looking around her. "It is autumn now. I must hurry."

It began to snow and Gerda's feet were cold and sore from walking. She sat down to rest when, all of a sudden, a large crow hopped up.

"Caw! Caw!" he said. "Where are you going to all alone?" Gerda told him her story and asked if he'd seen Kay.

"I expect he is with the princess. He has probably forgotten you by now," said the crow, flapping his wings and hopping from foot to foot.

"What do you mean?" asked Gerda. "What princess?"

"In the kingdom where we are now lives a very clever princess," began the crow. "One day, she decided to find a handsome and intelligent husband. A proclamation was sent out, inviting every good-looking young man to come for an interview. Straight away, crowds of young men rushed to the palace but none were chosen on the first day, or the second. The trouble was, when they saw the beauty of the princess they became tongue-tied. All they did was repeat what she had just said!"

"But when did Kay come?" asked Gerda.

"On the third day," replied the crow, "a boy came marching up to the palace. He had no horse or coach but carried a bag on his back."

"That must have been Kay!" cried Gerda. "But it was his sledge, not a bag."

"I heard the story from my sweetheart, who lives in the palace," said the crow. "The boy walked past the bodyguard, through the gold and silver rooms and straight up to the throne. His boots were new and squeaky, but he didn't mind. He marched straight up to the princess, who was sitting on a huge pearl."

"Kay had new boots!" said Gerda, "and is afraid of no one!"

"My sweetheart, the palace crow, says the boy was polite and pleasant to the princess and so very clever! She soon realised that he had not come to impress her, but to see how much he liked her. They fell in love instantly and were married the next day."

"Oh, it must be Kay!" said Gerda. "Please take me to the palace!" she begged.

"I can take you there, but it will be difficult to smuggle you inside. Let me first speak to my sweetheart. Wait here and I will return as soon as I can," said the crow.

Gerda waited all day until the crow returned.

"Caw! Caw!" he said. "My sweetheart sends you her love, and asked me to bring you a present," and he dropped a bread roll into her lap.

It was dark when they got to the palace. Gerda's heart was beating fast with excitement as the crow led her in through a back door. His sweetheart was waiting for them on a dark staircase lit by a small lamp.

"Take the lamp, Miss," said the palace crow, "I will go in front. No one will see us if we go this way." And off they set down a dark corridor.

"Somebody is behind us!" murmured Gerda, as whispering shadows of horses with flying manes danced on the walls.

"They are only dreams," said the crow, "carrying the prince and princess off to sleep."

At last they came into a magnificent bed-chamber. The walls

Hans Christian Andersen

"THE BOY WAS POLITE AND PLEASANT TO THE PRINCESS AND SO VERY CLEVER!"

were hung with rose-coloured satin and the ceiling was a canopy of crystal palm leaves. In the middle of the chamber, in two beds shaped like water lilies, lay the sleeping prince and princess. Gerda crept to the prince's bed and softly called Kay's name. The dreams went rushing from the chamber and the prince awoke – but Gerda could see that he was not Kay. She began to cry and wakened the princess, who asked what the matter was. Gerda told her story. When she finished, the prince and princess promised to help her and to reward the kind crows.

The prince climbed out of bed and insisted that Gerda spend the rest of the night there. As she drifted into sleep, the dreams came rustling and hissing back into the room. Gerda imagined she saw angels pulling a little sledge with Kay sitting on it. Next day, she was dressed in silk and velvet, a little fur muff and a pair of boots, and a golden coach took her on her journey.

There were sweet cakes, fruit and gingerbread-nuts for Gerda to eat as she travelled. The kind crows flew alongside her for the first few miles and then perched on a tree by the road, flapping their wings until the coach was out of sight. Soon the golden coach entered a dark forest. A band of robbers watched it and as it passed their hiding place they rushed out and seized the horses. They dragged Gerda out of the coach. "She looks as plump and juicy as a little lamb," said an old robber woman clutching a glittering knife.

"You mustn't kill her," said a robber-girl. "She must give me her muff and her pretty dress. Then she can play with me and sleep in my bed." The little robber-girl turned to Gerda. "They won't kill you unless I say so," she said. "Are you a princess?" Gerda told her the story of her search for Kay and the robber-girl listened silently.

At the robbers' castle, Gerda was led into a big smoky hall with a fire burning on the stone floor. A large cauldron of soup was boiling over it, and rabbits were being roasted on spits. After they had eaten, the robber-girl took Gerda to a corner covered with straw and carpets.

"Those are my wild doves," she said, pointing to a cage. "They'd fly away if they weren't locked up. And here is my dear old reindeer!" And she grabbed the poor reindeer by his antlers and dragged him towards Gerda.

"I keep him tied up so that he can't escape, and tickle his neck each night with my sharp knife, just to remind him that he is mine."

Gerda and the robber-girl lay down to sleep.

"You must tell me your story again!" the robber-girl ordered, clutching her knife in one hand. But once she was asleep and snoring loudly, the wild doves cooed to Gerda, "We have seen Kay. He was in the Snow Queen's sleigh when it flew over the forest. They were going to Lapland."

"Lapland is my home," said the reindeer. "The Snow Queen flies there each summer."

Next morning Gerda told the robber-girl what the doves and the reindeer had said. The robber-girl thought for a moment. "Wait until noon when all the men have gone out hunting and my mother takes a nap. Then I will help you," she said.

Once her mother was fast asleep, the little robber-girl went over to the reindeer.

"Much as I would love to keep you here and tickle you with my sharp knife," she said, "I am going to let you go back to Lapland. You must take Gerda to the Snow Queen's palace to find Kay." Then she lifted Gerda onto his back, tying her in place so that she wouldn't fall.

"You can keep your boots," she said, "but I want your pretty muff. Take my mother's gloves to keep your hands warm." And so saying, the robber-girl cut the rope that imprisoned the reindeer.

The Snow Queen

"'SHE LOOKS AS PLUMP AND JUICY AS A LITTLE LAMB,' SAID AN OLD ROBBER WOMAN CLUTCHING A GLITTERING KNIFE"

"Away you go!" she cried, "and take good care of Gerda." Gerda hugged the robber-girl goodbye and the reindeer galloped away through the gloomy forest.

They travelled for many days and nights, but when the night sky came alive with the dancing colours of the Northern Lights they knew they had reached Lapland. They stopped at a miserable-looking house with such a low door that they had to crawl in on all fours. Inside, an old woman sat by a stove cooking fish. Gerda was so cold that she could not speak, so the reindeer told her story as well as his own.

"Why you poor creatures," said the old woman, "the Snow Queen's summer palace is in Finland, hundreds of miles away." She gave them food and drink, and wrote a message on a piece of dried fish.

"Give this message to the Finnish wise-woman and I promise she will help you," she said. And she lifted Gerda onto the reindeer's back and wished them a safe journey.

All night long they flew like the wind until at last they came to the wise-woman's snow-house in Finland. She read the message. The reindeer repeated their story and asked the wise-woman for a magic potion strong enough to conquer the Snow Queen and rescue Kay. The wise-woman studied a parchment covered with strange writing.

At length she said, "Gerda already has more power than I can give her. Her tender heart and her innocence will protect her. You must carry her to the Snow Queen's garden and leave her near the bush covered with red berries. Then she must go alone to find the Snow Queen and Kay and remove the glass from his eye and his heart."

The wise-woman put Gerda on the reindeer's back and he galloped away as fast as he could. Gerda had forgotten her boots and her mittens and it was freezing cold, but they did not stop until they

The Snow Queen

KAY AND THE SNOW QUEEN

reached the bush with the red berries. The reindeer set her down and kissed her with tears in his eyes before cantering away. A snowstorm swirled towards Gerda but the flakes were running along the ground instead of falling from the sky, and the closer they came the larger they grew. They were shaped like strange animals. Some were like white porcupines, some like coiled snakes and others like fierce, growling bears. Gerda was frightened and she began saying her prayers. As she spoke, the warm breath from her mouth looked like clouds of steam, and the clouds changed into hunters and warriors armed with spears and shields. They drove away the snow animals, and Gerda hurried on towards the Snow Queen's palace.

The walls of the palace were made of snowdrifts and the windows and doors were howling winds. Inside, the rooms were lit by the flashing Northern Lights but they were icy cold, empty and frightening. In the middle of the biggest snow-hall was a frozen lake on which the ice was cracked into a thousand pieces, each one exactly the same as the others. In the centre of the lake sat the Snow Queen who called it her Mirror of Reason, the only mirror that showed the world as it really was. And there was poor Kay! He was blue with cold but he felt nothing. The kisses of the Snow Queen had robbed him of all feeling. He was dragging around some blocks of ice, hopelessly trying to form them into patterns. To him it seemed the most important thing in the world.

"You shall have your freedom," the Snow Queen had told him, "if you can make the word 'Eternity' out of the blocks of ice." But however hard poor Kay tried, he couldn't do it.

"It is time for me to visit the warm countries," said the Snow Queen. "I shall whiten the mountain tops and sprinkle frost on the lemons and grapes to kill them." She flew off, leaving Kay all alone. And this was how Gerda found him, sitting still and stiff with cold.

The Snow Queen

"Kay! Dear Kay! I have found you at last!" she cried and put her arms round him. Her warm tears flowed over him and soaked into his heart and the ice of the Snow Queen's kisses were melted.

He turned his eyes towards Gerda and smiled. Together they sang their special song from the summer:

"The roses bloom for just one hour, then die;

but go on living evermore, on high."

Kay burst into tears and the sliver of glass was washed out of his eye.

"Gerda! Beloved Gerda! Where have you been? And where have I been?" he cried, looking around. Laughing and crying, the children hugged one another and as they did so the blocks of ice formed themselves into the word "Eternity". Kay was freed for ever from the power of the Snow Queen.

Hand-in-hand, Gerda and Kay made their way out of the Snow Queen's terrible ice-palace. They talked about home and of the beautiful roses growing from the window boxes. Wherever they walked, the bitter winds died away and the sun shone. The reindeer was waiting for them with a female reindeer, who gave the children her warm milk to drink. Then they carried Gerda and Kay to the wise-woman's snow-home and from there to Lapland, where the old woman gave them new clothes and took them by sledge to the border country.

Gerda and Kay waved goodbye to them all and set off on foot through a forest filled with green buds and singing birds. They met a girl on horseback, and it was none other than the little robber-girl.

"So this is the silly boy you have rescued from the end of the world," she laughed. "I hope he is grateful to you." Gerda hugged the robber-girl and asked if she had news of the prince and princess and the crows.

"The royal couple are travelling in foreign lands," said the robber-girl, "but your wild crow is dead and his sweetheart is very upset. But do tell me everything that's happened." Gerda and Kay told the robber-girl all their adventures before they said goodbye, promising they would never forget each other.

The further Kay and Gerda travelled onwards, the greener and more beautiful the landscape became until finally, one morning, they heard the sound of church bells ringing and saw their own village in the distance. They walked together through the familiar streets to Grandmother's door and went up the stairs.

Nothing in the old room seemed to have changed. But one thing was very different. When they looked at one another, Gerda and Kay realised that they were now grown-up. The roses were blooming in the window boxes and in the garden. They sat on the little chairs they had used as children and held hands, while the icy, empty splendour of the Snow Queen's palace melted from their memory.

Grandmother sat reading in the warm sunshine, and Kay and Gerda looked at one another. They were grown up now, but in their hearts they were still children. They began to sing happily together:

"The roses bloom for just one hour, then die;
but go on living evermore, on high."

The Snow Queen

THE NIGHTINGALE

Many years ago in China, there was an emperor who ruled over the land and its people. The emperor's palace was the most splendid in the world. It was made entirely of expensive porcelain and it was so delicate that the people had to be careful how they touched it. In the garden were the most wonderful flowers, and to the most expensive of them there had been tied tiny silver bells that rang when people passed by. Everything in the emperor's garden was beautifully arranged. It was so big that even the gardener could not tell where it ended. If a man walked on and on eventually he would come to a glorious forest with tall trees and a deep, clear lake. The wood extended down to the sea, which was brilliant blue. Great ships sailed beneath the branches of the trees, and in these trees lived a nightingale. The nightingale sang so beautifully that even the poor

The Nightingale

fisherman, who was busy throwing out his nets, stopped still and listened to his song.

"How beautiful that is!" he cried, but he had so much to do that he got back to work and forgot the bird. But the next day the fisherman heard the nightingale's song once more and again cried, "How beautiful that is!"

Travellers came from all over the world to admire the emperor's city, and they marvelled at the palace and the garden. But when they heard the nightingale's song they said, "That's the best wonder of all!"

When the travellers returned home, they would tell people all about the emperor's city, the palace and the garden, but they did not forget the nightingale, which they placed highest of all. Wise men wrote books and poets wrote magnificent poems about the nightingale in the wood by the deep, clear lake.

The books spread all around the world, and eventually some came to the emperor. He sat on his golden throne and read and read. With every beautiful description of his city, the palace and the garden he nodded his head in agreement. "But the nightingale is the best wonder of all," it was written at the end.

"What's this?" exclaimed the emperor. "I don't know of this nightingale! Is there such a bird in my empire, in my own garden, that I have never heard of? How can it be that I am learning this from a book?"

The emperor called for his most honourable court gentleman. The courtier was so grand that if anyone lowlier than him dared speak to him he simply answered "P!" which meant nothing.

"I have never heard of him," replied the courtier. "He has never been introduced at court."

"I command that the nightingale comes to the palace this

evening to sing for me," said the emperor. "The whole world knows what I possess, but I don't know it myself!"

"I've never heard anyone talk about it," said the courtier, "but I will find it."

The courtier ran up and down all the staircases in the palace, through halls and corridors, but no one in the palace had met or even heard of the nightingale. He ran back to the emperor and said that the nightingale could be a story invented by writers.

"Your Majesty, a lot of fiction is written about our land, perhaps someone made up the story of the nightingale," said the courtier.

"But the book was sent to me by the high and mighty Emperor of Japan," said the emperor, "so it must be true. I will hear the nightingale! It must be here this evening! It has been commanded by its emperor, and if it does not come then I will arrange for all the courtiers to be trampled upon after dinner!"

"Tsing-pe!" said the courtier, and again he ran up and down all the staircases in the palace and through all the halls and corridors. Half of the courtiers ran with him because they did not want to be trampled upon.

There was a big investigation into the nightingale, which all the world knew about except the emperor and his courtiers. Finally, the courtiers met a poor little girl in the kitchen, who said, "The nightingale? Yes, I know him well; he can sing gloriously. Every evening I am allowed to take my poor sick mother the scraps from the table. When I get back I am tired and I rest in the wood, where I listen to the nightingale sing until tears come to my eyes, just as if my mother had kissed me."

"Little kitchen girl," said the courtier, "I will promote you to chef and let you watch the emperor dine if you will take us to the nightingale. The emperor wants him to sing at the palace this evening."

The Nightingale

So the girl led half the courtiers to the wood where the nightingale sang. On the way, a cow began to low in the nearby field.

"That's him!" cried one of the pages. "What wonderful power for such a small creature! I have definitely heard this song before."

"No, that is a cow lowing!" said the kitchen girl. "We are still a long way from the place where the nightingale sings."

The frogs began to croak in the marsh.

"Glorious!" said the preacher. "I can hear him – he sounds just like the bells in the temple."

"No, those are frogs!" said the kitchen girl. "But I think we'll hear him soon."

The nightingale began to sing.

"That's him!" cried the kitchen girl. "Listen, he's nearby."

She pointed to a little, grey bird up in the tree.

"Can it be possible," said the courtier, "that he looks that simple and plain? He must have lost his colour after seeing us all dressed so grandly."

"Little nightingale!" called the kitchen girl. "Our gracious emperor wants you to sing for him."

"It would be my pleasure!" replied the nightingale, and he began to sing the most delightful song.

"He sounds like glass bells!" said the courtier. It's unbelievable that we've never heard him before. The bird will be a great success."

"Shall I sing for the emperor again?" asked the nightingale, because he thought that the emperor was there.

"My excellent nightingale," said the courtier. "I have great pleasure in inviting you to a festival at the palace this evening, where you shall charm his Majesty with your beautiful singing."

"My song sounds best in the woods," replied the nightingale, "but I will come if the emperor would like me to."

The palace was decorated for the festival. The porcelain walls and floors gleamed in the light of a thousand golden lamps, and the most glorious of all the flowers, the ones that rang the most beautifully, were brought in from the garden and placed in the corridors. There was a lot of running around, which caused such a draught that the bells rang too loudly and no one could hear themselves speak.

The emperor sat on his throne in the great hall. In the middle of the room was a golden perch for the nightingale to sit on. All the courtiers were there and the little kitchen girl, who had been promoted to the title of Court Chef, stood behind the door. Everyone was dressed in wonderful robes and they all looked at the little, grey bird.

The nightingale sang so gloriously that tears came to the emperor's eyes and ran down his cheeks. Then the nightingale sang even more sweetly and the sound went straight to the emperor's heart. The emperor was so pleased that he offered the nightingale his golden slipper to wear around his neck. But the nightingale said that he had been given reward enough.

"I have seen tears in the emperor's eyes – that is the greatest treasure of all. An emperor's tears are very special, and that is enough reward for me." With that, he began to sing again.

"That is the best flattery I have ever heard!" cried the ladies of the court, and they tried to imitate the nightingale by filling their mouths with water and gurgling whenever a gentleman spoke to them. Even the chamber maids were pleased with the singing, and they were the hardest of all to impress. As the courtier had predicted, the nightingale was a great success.

The Nightingale

"THE ARTIFICIAL BIRD HAS ITS PLACE ON A SILKEN CUSHION
CLOSE TO THE EMPEROR'S BED"

The nightingale was ordered to remain at court. He had his own cage and was allowed to go out twice each day and once at night. Twelve servants accompanied him when he went out, each of whom held tight to a string of silk fastened to the bird's leg. There was no joy for the poor nightingale.

The whole city talked of the wonderful bird. Children were even named after him, though none of them could sing a note.

One day, the emperor received a parcel, which had the words "The Nightingale" written on it.

"Ah, a new book all about my wonderful bird," said the emperor.

But it was not a book; it was a wonderful work of art. The emperor had been sent an artificial nightingale, which was decorated with diamonds, rubies and sapphires and could sing like a real bird. When the bird was wound up it sang a beautiful song and its tail moved up and down. As it moved, it shone with silver and gold.

"They must sing together!" cried the emperor. "What a duet it will be!"

So the two birds sang together, but it did not sound good. The real nightingale sang its own song while the artificial nightingale sang waltzes.

"It's not the artificial bird's fault," said the play-write, "it's lovely and I like its song."

The emperor ordered that the artificial bird should sing alone. It was just as successful as the real one and it was prettier to look at. It sang its song thirty-three times and was still not tired. The people loved to hear it, but the emperor ordered that the real nightingale should sing a song next. But no one had noticed that he had flown out of a window, back to the green wood.

"Why would the nightingale do such a thing?" asked the emperor.

The Nightingale

With that, the courtiers declared that the nightingale was an ungrateful creature.

"We have the best bird," they said.

The courtiers listened to the artificial bird's song for the thirty-fourth time and they still did not know it from heart because it was so intricate. The play-write praised the artificial bird and declared that it was better than the real one, not only because it looked better, but inside as well.

"Your Majesty, ladies and gentlemen, a real nightingale is unpredictable, but the artificial one is very settled. We can open it and explain it, to make people understand where waltzes come from and how they go."

"We agree!" said the rest of the courtiers.

The emperor commanded that, on Sunday, the people of the city should hear the bird sing. The people were delighted with its song, but the poor fisherman, who had heard the real nightingale, said, "It sounds nice enough, but there's something missing, though I don't know what."

The real nightingale was banished from the Empire, while the artificial bird took its place on a silk cushion next to the emperor's bed. It was surrounded by heaps of gold and precious stones, which it had received as gifts. It had earned the title of High Imperial After-Dinner-Singer and was ranked higher than anyone in the court. The play-write wrote twenty-five volumes about it, which were very long and difficult, and everyone in the city declared that they had read and understood them because no one wanted to look stupid.

A year went by and the emperor, the court and all the people of the empire knew every twitter off by heart. They loved it because they could sing along, and even the emperor joined in.

But one evening, when the artificial bird was singing at its best, and the emperor lay in bed listening to it, something inside it went "Whizz!" and something cracked. "Whir-r-r!" it went as all the wheels spun round and the music stopped.

The emperor sprang out of bed and called the palace doctor. But he couldn't do anything. So the emperor sent for the watchmaker and, after a lot of talking and investigation, the bird was almost fixed. The watchmaker warned that the bird must be treated carefully because the barrels inside it had worn and it would be impossible to replace them. It was to sing only once a year and even that was almost too much. The people were upset until the play-write made a little speech, full of heavy words, and convinced them that things were as good as before.

Five years went by and sorrow fell upon the Empire. The people loved their emperor, but he was very ill and they feared that he would not live much longer. A new emperor had been selected, yet the people in the street still asked the courtier how their emperor was.

"P!" he said, and he shook his head.

The emperor lay cold, stiff and pale on his luxurious bed. The courtiers all thought that he had died and they rushed to welcome their new ruler. The maids even had a tea party. Cloth had been laid in all the corridors so that no footstep could be heard, and so the palace had fallen silent. But the emperor was not yet dead; he simply lay there resting, surrounded by his expensive velvet curtains and gold tassels. An open window above the bed allowed the moonlight to shine down on to the emperor and the artificial bird.

The emperor could hardly breathe. He opened his eyes and saw that Death was lying upon his chest. It had put on his golden crown, and it held his sword in one hand and his beautiful banner in the other. All around, in the folds of the splendid velvet curtains, strange

The Nightingale

heads appeared; some ugly and some soft and beautiful. They were the emperor's good and bad deeds.

"Do you remember this?" whispered one to another. "Do you remember that?" and then they talked and talked until the emperor broke out in a sweat.

"I did not know that!" shouted the emperor. "Play music! Play the great Chinese drum!" he cried. "Please drown out the voices!"

But they carried on talking and Death nodded to everything they said.

"Sing! You precious golden bird, sing!" cried the emperor. "I have given you gold and expensive presents, and even hung my gold slipper around your neck. Sing now!"

But the bird stood still. No one was there to wind it up and it could not sing without that. Death continued to stare at the emperor with its large, hollow eyes, and the palace was fearfully quiet.

All of a sudden, there was a beautiful sound and a lovely song could be heard. The nightingale was sitting outside the window. He had heard of the emperor's plight and had come to sing his hopeful and comforting song. As he sang, the heads faded and the blood in the emperor's body ran faster through his limbs. Even Death listened and said, "Go on, little nightingale, go on."

"Only if you give me the emperor's golden crown, his sword and his banner."

So Death gave up the treasures for the song, and the nightingale sang on and on. He sang all about the churchyard where white roses grow and where the blossom smells sweet and where the grass is wet with mourners' tears. Death longed to see its churchyard garden and it floated out of the window in a cold, white mist.

Hans Christian Andersen

" 'Music! music!' cried the emperor. 'You little precious golden bird, sing!' "

"Thank you! Thank you!" said the emperor. "You heavenly bird! I banished you from my Empire and yet you still charmed away the evil faces and banished Death from my heart. How can I reward you?"

"You have rewarded me!" replied the nightingale. "I received my reward when I drew tears from your eyes the first time I sang for you. I shall never forget that. That is the best reward a singer can receive. Now sleep and grow strong again. I will sing for you." The bird sang and the emperor fell into a sweet slumber. The sun shone in upon him through the windows, and he awoke refreshed and restored. None of his servants had returned; only the nightingale still sat beside him.

"You must always stay with me," said the emperor. "Sing as you wish to and I'll break the artificial bird into a thousand pieces."

"No," said the nightingale, "it did as well as it could, so you should continue to look after it. I can't build my nest in the palace but I shall come and sing for you when I want to. I'll sing for those who are happy and those who are sad, and of the good and evil that surrounds you. Singing birds must fly all around and sing to the poor fisherman and to the peasant's roof, and to all those who live far away from you and your palace. I love your kind heart more than I love your crown. I will sing for you, but you must promise me one thing."

"Anything! Everything!" cried the emperor.

"Promise me that you will not tell anyone that you have a bird who sings you everything. That will make things much easier." And the nightingale flew away.

The servants returned to look at their dead emperor and found him standing in front of them in good health. "Good morning!" he said.

THE LITTLE MATCH GIRL

It was New Year's Eve. A little girl was wandering barefoot and alone through the freezing, snowy streets. When she left home, she had been wearing slippers, but they were too big for her small feet and had fallen off as she stumbled over the frozen ruts. A boy had pounced on one and run off with it, and the other had been lost in the snow. The little girl carried a small bundle of matches. She had been trying to sell them all day long, but nobody wanted them and she had not earned one single penny. Shivering and hungry, she crept along on her blue, frozen feet. Light streamed from all the windows and the smell of roast goose filled the air, but she hardly noticed.

At last, she sat down against a wall, tucking her feet beneath her to try and warm them. If she went home, her father would beat her for not selling anything and besides, it was cold there too. The wind

The Little Match Girl

howled into their tiny attic through holes in the roof, even though they were stuffed with rags.

The little girl fumbled for a match from the bunch in her frozen fingers. At last, she pulled one out and struck it against the wall. It sparked and burned and its warm, bright flame was like a little candle. The little girl felt safe and cosy, as if she was sitting by a big iron stove with a fire blazing in its grate. But when she stretched out her feet to warm them the flame vanished, and she was left holding a half-burned match.

The little girl struck another match and, as it flared, it lit the wall and seemed to make it transparent so that she could see into the room behind. She saw a large table spread with a snow-white cloth and smelled a delicious dish of roast goose stuffed with apples. Suddenly, the roast goose jumped down from the dish and came waddling over to the poor little girl. Then the match went out and she saw nothing but the cold, damp wall. She lit another match and found herself sitting under a tall Christmas tree, the finest she had ever seen. A thousand candles lit up the gold and silver baubles that hung from the green branches. Then the match went out.

The little girl looked up at the twinkling stars and saw one fall and leave a fiery trail. She knew that a falling star is the sign of a soul going up to heaven.

"Somebody is dying," she thought, and remembered her grandmother, the only person who had ever loved her and who was now dead.

She struck another match on the wall and in the brightness of the flame she saw her grandmother's loving face appear before her.

"Grandmother," she cried, "take me with you! I'm afraid you will vanish when the match goes out!"

Hans Christian Andersen

"In the brightness the old grandmother stood"

The Little Match Girl

She wanted to cuddle her grandmother so much that she picked up a whole handful of matches and struck them hard against the wall. The light seemed to blaze brighter than the sun itself and the grandmother took the little girl into her arms and flew upwards with her to heaven, where she would never be cold or hungry or unloved again.

Next morning, when people found the body of the little girl, still holding the burned matches, they said, "See how she tried to warm herself."

But nobody could ever know the magic wonders she had seen or imagine the happiness she had felt when she was cradled in her grandmother's arms at last.

THE ELF HILL

Three large lizards raced nimbly around an old tree, chatting to each other.

"The elf hill is so noisy!" said one lizard. "I haven't been able to sleep for two nights because it's so loud!"

"Something's going on in there," said the second lizard. "They are airing the hill every few days and the elf girls have all learned new dances."

"Yes, I spoke to an earthworm yesterday – one of my good friends," said the third lizard. "He had just left the hill, where he had been all day and night, and he had heard everything. He can't see anything, the poor thing, but he can hear very well. The elves are expecting a visit from some very wealthy strangers, but the earthworm wouldn't tell me who they are. All the jack-o-lanterns have been told to hold a torch dance, and all the silver and gold in the elf hill is being polished and put out in the moonlight."

"I wonder who these strangers are," said the lizards. "What can be going on in the elf hill? It hums and murmurs all day long."

At that moment, the elf hill opened and an old elf lady came out. She was the elf king's housekeeper and she tripped up every few steps. She was a distant relative of the royal family and she wore an amber heart on her head. She moved quickly, tripping as she went, and made her way down to the sea to where the night raven lived.

"You are invited to the elf hill this evening," said the old elf lady to the night raven, "but you are to send the rest of the invitations. We are going to have some very special guests and the king wants to make a good impression."

"Who should I invite?" asked the night raven.

"The whole world can come – even men – as long as they are like us in some way. Before the party there will be a feast but only the most important guests should be invited to it. Not even the ghosts can come. The first people to invite are the merman and his daughters – they don't like dry land, but we'll give them a wet stone to sit on and some gifts so that they can't refuse. Invite all the oldest and wealthiest demons – the ones with tails – as well as the wood demon and his gnomes. I don't think we can forget the clergy – the grave pig, the death horse, and the church twig. They may not be like us, but they always make the effort to visit and so they are part of our community.

"Croak!" said the night raven, and it flew off to deliver the invitations.

The elf girls were dressed in pretty shawls woven from mist and moonlight, and they were dancing on the elf hill. Below the hill, the great hall had been beautifully decorated; the floor had been washed with moonlight, and the walls had been rubbed with witches' balm so they glowed like tulips in the light. In the kitchen, frogs were being roasted; snails and children's fingers were being baked; and salads of mushroom, mouse and hemlock were being prepared. The witch had brewed some beer, and there were bowls of sweets mixed with rusty nails and church window glass. The elf king's crown had been polished using the finest powdered slate, and the curtains were fastened open with snail slime. Everything looked splendid.

"We have to burn some horsehair and pig bristle incense," said the elf king, "and then we'll have finished."

"Father," said his youngest daughter, "now will you tell me who our special guests are?"

"Well," said the elf king, "I suppose I can tell you now. My dear daughters, two of you must get married. The old gnome from the Dovre Mountains in Norway is coming with two of his sons and each will choose one of you to be his wife. The gnome owns a large gold mine and many fine castles. He's an honest and merry gnome – I met him many years ago when he came here to find himself a wife. We were young and enjoyed drinking together. In the end he married a daughter of the King of Chalk-rocks of Moen, and they were happily married until she died. I can't wait to see him again. I hear that his sons are rather rude, but I'm sure they'll mature and maybe you will be able to teach them some manners."

"When are they coming?" asked the daughters.

"That depends on the weather," said the elf king. "They are travelling by boat. I advised them to travel by land, but the old gnome is very traditional, stubborn even, and he refused."

Two jack-o-lanterns came hopping over.

"They're coming! They're coming!" they cried.

The Elf Hill

"THEY DANCED WITH SHAWLS WHICH WERE WOVEN OF MIST AND MOONSHINE"

"Pass me my crown, and let me stand in the moonlight," said the elf king.

The daughters lifted their shawls and bowed to their special guests.

There stood the old gnome of Dovre, wearing a crown of ice and polished fir cones, a bearskin and furry boots. His sons looked very strong. They had bare necks and wore trousers.

"You call that a hill?" asked the youngest son, and he pointed at the elf hill. "At home in Norway we'd call that a hole!"

"Boys! Don't be rude!" said the old gnome. "Holes go down, mounds go up. Don't you have eyes?"

"Don't worry father," said one of the sons, "I'd be surprised if these elves can even understand what we're saying. They look pretty daft."

"Don't be bigheaded," said the old gnome. "You're no better than they are."

They all went into the elf hill, where the most respected guests had gathered. The sea-people sat in large baths and said it was just like being at home. Everyone was polite at dinner, except the young gnomes. They put their feet up on the table – just because they felt like it.

"Get your feet off the table cloth!" cried the old gnome.

The sons reluctantly did as they were told. But then they tickled the ladies with pine cones, and took off their boots and made the ladies hold them. The old Dovre gnome was very different; he told charming stories about the proud Norwegian rocks and of the waterfalls that rushed over them, with their bright white foam. He told how the water sounded like thunder and church organs, and how the salmon would leap upstream against the current. He told of

The Elf Hill

" 'DON'T GIVE YOURSELF AIRS,' SAID THE OLD MAN "

shining winter nights when the sleigh bells would jingle, and how the boys would run around on the ice, which was so transparent that they could see the fish dart around underneath. He told the stories so well that his listeners could see the rocks and the waterfall before them. The servants and the maids were singing and dancing, and all at once, in the excitement of the evening, the gnome gave the old elf lady a kiss.

The elf ladies started to dance, with wonderful movements and graceful steps. They danced so fast that it was hard to tell where they started and where they ended, or which were their arms and which were their legs. They whirled around and around until the grave pig and the death horse felt so dizzy that they had to go home.

"Prur!" said the old gnome, "that's unusual dancing! But what else can they do?"

"You shall soon see!" said the elf king.

Then he called his youngest daughter forward. She was as light and as graceful as moonlight, and she was the most delicate of all the sisters. She put a white shaving in her mouth, and suddenly she disappeared. That was her trick.

But the old gnome said that he would not want a wife who could disappear, and he did not think his sons would, either.

The second youngest daughter could walk under herself, as if she had a shadow, which none of the gnomes had. The third daughter had worked in the witch's brewery and knew how to stuff tree knots with glow-worms.

"She'd be a good housewife," said the old gnome.

Next was the fourth daughter. She brought out a huge harp. When she played her first chord all the gnomes lifted up their left leg, and by the time she struck her second chord all the gnomes were under her spell and would do exactly as she wished.

The Elf Hill

"That's a dangerous woman!" cried the old gnome.

Both the sons had grown bored and had wandered outside.

"What can the next daughter do?" asked the old gnome.

"I love everything that is Norwegian," she said, "and I won't marry unless I can go to Norway."

But the youngest daughter whispered to the old gnome, "That's only because she's heard in an old song that when the world sinks only the cliffs of Norway will remain standing. She only wants to go because she's scared of sinking!"

"Oh, I see!" said the old gnome. "What can the seventh daughter do?"

"You forgot number six!" said the elf king. The old gnome was not good at counting.

But the sixth daughter would not come out.

"All I can do is tell the truth!" she said. "Nobody wants me and I am very busy sewing."

Finally, out came the seventh daughter. She could tell as many wonderful stories as people wanted to hear.

"Here are all my fingers," said the old gnome, "tell me a story for each."

So she took him by the wrist and told stories until the old gnome was in fits of laughter. When she came to the ring finger, which already had a ring around it – almost as if by magic, the old gnome said, "Enough! My hand is yours; I would like you to be my own wife!"

"But I haven't told a story for the ring finger or the fifth finger," she said.

"We'll hear those in winter," said the old gnome, "and we'll hear about the pine tree, and the birch tree, and about the spirits' gifts and about the biting frost. You're the best storyteller in the world! We'll sit in a stone house, with a warm fire and drink sweet mead. We'll be so happy and the salmon will leap in the stream."

"Living in Norway sounds wonderful," said the daughter, "but where are your sons?"

They were running around in the fields blowing out the jack-o-lanterns, which were lighting the torch dance.

"What kind of behaviour is that?" said the old gnome. "I have found a mother for you, and now you can choose one of the aunts."

But the sons said they would rather drink and have fun than get married. They talked and drank all night, and afterwards they fell asleep on the table. The old gnome danced with his new bride and they swapped boots, which in those days was more fashionable than swapping rings.

"The cock is crowing," said the old elf lady, "it's time to close the shutters so we don't get burnt by the sun."

So the elf hill shut itself up. Outside, the lizards ran up and down the tree and said, "I like that old Norwegian gnome!"

"I prefer the sons," said the earthworm. But that was because the poor thing couldn't see.

The Elf Hill

THE LITTLE MERMAID

Far away, deep down under the sea where the water is crystal clear and as blue as cornflowers, live the sea-folk. On the sea floor a forest of strange trees and flowers sways back and forth, with fish gliding among them like birds riding the wind. In the deepest spot stands the sea-king's palace; it has walls of coral, windows of clear amber and a roof of seashells, each holding a priceless pearl.

The sea-king's wise old mother looked after the palace, and the six pretty little princess-mermaids. The youngest, with her delicate soft skin and sea-blue eyes, was the loveliest.

All day long, the little princesses played in the underwater palace and fed and stroked the fishes that swam in and out of the amber windows. Each princess had a garden in which she planted flowers and made decorations from things found in shipwrecks.

The Little Mermaid

On calm days the mermaids looked up and saw the sun above the blue waters, like a shining flower with petals of light. The youngest mermaid planted her garden in a circle like the sun, with flowers of the same red colour. In the middle she placed the pretty marble statue of a boy that she had found on the seabed after a shipwreck. She also grew a weeping-willow tree and, as it got bigger, its branches wound round the statue and reached down to the fine yellow sand. The little mermaid loved listening to her grandmother's stories about the world above the sea, where flowers smelled of perfume and birds sang in the trees.

"On your fifteenth birthday," said her grandmother, "you will be allowed to swim up to the surface and sit on the rocks in the moonlight. Then you will see the ships, towns and forests."

The eldest princess would soon be fifteen, but the rest were younger and it would be a long time before the little mermaid, the youngest of them all, had her chance to see the world. At night she could think of little else and would stand gazing upwards through the dark, blue water. She would see the pale moon and the twinkling stars, and watch the fish as they swam. When a black shadow went gliding overhead she knew it might be a ship full of people, and she would stretch up her arms towards it.

On the eldest mermaid's birthday, she swam to the surface of the sea. When she returned, she told them all she had seen.

"I lay on a sandbank in the calm sea," she said, "and gazed at a city with shining lights. I heard music playing and people talking and church bells ringing."

The youngest mermaid went to the open window and looked up towards the surface. She thought about the busy city and imagined she could hear the church bells.

In a year's time, it was the second sister's turn to swim to the surface. She told her sisters about the sunset that turned the sky gold, the clouds violet and the sun rose-red.

The third sister swam up a river and saw vine-covered hills, woods and castles. She heard birds singing and felt the warm sun, and saw human children playing in the water. She swam towards them to join in, but they ran away and a dog barked fiercely at her. The younger mermaid longed to see the beauty of the setting sun, but most of all she wanted to watch human children playing.

The fourth sister rose in the middle of the ocean and watched dolphins turn somersaults, whales blow fountains of water and ships sail by.

It was winter when the fifth sister's turn came. Huge icebergs, bigger than cathedrals built by humans, floated like diamonds in the green sea. She sat on the biggest of them and let the wind blow her long hair. She watched the ships begin to go faster as they sailed past, almost as though they were frightened of her. Towards evening, red and blue lightning lit the dark sky and illuminated the icebergs lifted high by the dark waves.

All five sisters were enchanted by the beauty of what they had seen above the sea, but even so they agreed that their own sea-world was even more beautiful. In the evenings, they would hold hands and rise to the surface singing. If a storm arose, they would swim down with the sinking ship, and sing sweetly to the sailors not to be afraid of the world below. But the sailors mistook the singing for the howling of the wind and drowned without seeing the sea-kingdom.

And all the time, the youngest sister watched and wanted to cry – but she couldn't because mermaids have no tears.

"How I wish I could be fifteen at once!" she sighed. "I know I shall love the world and all the people in it."

At long last, the little mermaid's fifteenth birthday arrived.

"Well, now you are grown up!" said her grandmother, as she put a headdress of pearls shaped like lilies in her hair, and servants fastened eight oyster shells to her tail to show that she was a princess. The little princess complained that the shells hurt and the headdress was heavy but, as her grandmother told her, "Pride must suffer pain."

As she lifted her head above the waves for the very first time, the sun was just setting and there were golden fringes around the pink clouds. A ship lay still on the calm sea. The little mermaid could see sailors sitting on deck and hear music and singing. When it was dark, hundreds of coloured lanterns were lit and the little mermaid swam up to a cabin window and peeped in. A celebration was going on: she saw people dressed in fine clothes and a handsome boy with large, dark eyes. He was a prince and this was his birthday party. Up on deck the sailors danced and, when the prince came to watch them, fireworks were lit and sparkled in the air. The little mermaid thought they were stars falling from the sky and dived under the water. When she came up she watched the dazzling fireworks light up the sky and the face of the handsome boy.

But in a while the clouds gathered and a terrible storm blew up. Although the sailors struggled to steer a course through the raging sea, the ship began to break up. At first, the little mermaid was pleased to see it sink, thinking the prince was coming to join her in her world. Then she remembered that humans cannot live in water and knew that somehow she must save him.

She swam towards him through the heavy beams and planks that were tumbling on the waves as the ship broke into pieces, and reached him just as he had given up his struggle against the sea. His eyes were closed and his arms and legs were still. The little mermaid held his head above the water and let the waves carry them all night.

By dawn, the storm was over, and not a single piece of the ship could be seen. The mermaid kissed the prince's head and stroked his wet hair. He seemed so like the marble statue in her garden and she wanted desperately to save him. Soon she saw land and, as they got nearer, the white convent of a church in a garden of lemon and orange trees. She swam to the shore and pushed the prince onto the sand, and then she went and hid behind some rocks. As she watched, a bell rang in the white convent and some young girls came out into the garden. Before long, one of them came to the shore and saw the prince. She went running back to fetch help, and soon the prince was carried away.

With a sigh, the sad little mermaid slid back into the water and swam down to her father's palace. When her sisters asked what she had seen, she would not tell them. She would often swim to the spot where she had left the prince in the hope of seeing him, but she never did. Her only comfort was to sit in her little garden with her arms around the beautiful statue.

At length, she could keep her secret to herself no longer and she told her sisters all about it. Now all the mermaids went searching for the handsome prince, and before long they found him.

"Come, little sister," they said, and holding hands they rose to the surface together at the very spot where the prince's palace stood.

It was a magnificent palace, built of shining yellow stone with a flight of marble steps that reached down to the sea. Through the large windows the mermaids could see splendid rooms decorated with beautiful wall-hangings and priceless paintings. In one room, a fountain shot sparkling jets of water towards a glass-domed ceiling, through which the sun shone.

Now that the little mermaid knew where the prince lived she visited the palace often, swimming nearer and nearer until she could gaze at his handsome face. She longed to be with him, and to belong

The Little Mermaid

to his world that seemed to her more beautiful than her own. She wanted to know everything about the lands above the sea and never stopped asking her grandmother questions.

"If human beings do not get drowned, does that mean they live for ever?" she asked one day.

"They die, just as we do," said her grandmother, "and they live shorter lives than ours. We can live to three hundred years but, when we die, we change into foam on the wave tops. Humans have souls that live on after their bodies are dead. They rise up beyond the stars to a place that no one has ever seen or known."

"I would happily change my long life for just one day as a human being if I had the hope of seeing that wonderful place," said the little mermaid sadly. "Is there nothing I can do to have a soul?"

"Nothing," said her old grandmother, "unless a human loves you enough to marry you and get the blessing of a priest. Then the human's soul will enter your body and give you a soul of your own. But that could never happen unless you could change your mermaid's tail into human legs."

That night there was a grand ball in the sea-king's palace. It was lit by hundreds of blue flames flickering in gigantic seashells. They shone through the glass walls, lighting up the sea all around and attracting countless tiny fishes, whose rainbow colours flashed and sparkled like liquid silver. The mermaids and mermen danced the night away to the sound of their own sweet singing. The little mermaid sang more sweetly than anyone else in the room, and everyone applauded her and she felt happy. But her thoughts soon went back to the upper world, and the handsome prince who might marry her and give her a soul. She crept away from the palace to sit in her little garden. Through the water, she thought she heard the sound of a trumpet and felt sure that the prince was sailing up above.

"I will risk everything to win him," thought the little mermaid. "The sea-witch must help me."

It was a dangerous journey to the sea-witch's house. First, the little mermaid had to pass rushing whirlpools that tried to suck her into their swirling depths. Then she had to cross great mud banks that heaved and bubbled all around her. She nearly turned back when she reached the ugly forest of half-animal, half-plant creatures with branches like long, slimy arms and grasping, worm-like fingers. But all the time she thought of the prince and of the human soul she would have. She pinned up her hair and darted through the wriggling forest until she reached a vast swamp. In the middle of the swamp stood a house built of human bones. Inside it sat the sea-witch, feeding a toad, with fat water-snakes coiled all around her.

"I know what you want little mermaid!" said the sea-witch. "And you are very stupid to want something that will plunge you into misfortune! But if you are determined to do it, I can prepare you a magic potion. Before sunrise tomorrow you must swim ashore and drink it. Your tail will shrivel away and human legs will grow, but it will be agony, as if a sharp sword is being thrust through you. When you walk, you will move like a beautiful dancer, but every step you take will be like treading on sharp knives. Are you prepared to suffer so much for a handsome prince and a human soul?"

"I am," said the little mermaid in a trembling voice.

"But be warned!" said the witch. "Once you have human form you can never be a mermaid again, and if the prince does not fall in love with you and marry you with a priest's blessing you will never obtain a human soul. If he marries another your heart will break, and the very next day you will dissolve into the foam on the sea."

The little mermaid turned deathly pale, but all she said was, "I understand your warning."

"In exchange for my magic potion, you must give me your most valuable possession," said the sea-witch. "You must give me your lovely voice."

"But if you take my voice," said the little mermaid, "what have I left?"

"You will still have your prettiness and your beautiful eyes," said the witch. "Are they not enough to capture a man's heart? Don't be afraid. Put out your tongue and let me cut it off and then you shall have the potion."

The sea-witch prepared the magic potion in her cauldron. When the boiling mixture was ready, it looked like pure spring water. The witch poured the sparkling liquid into a crystal bottle and cut off the little mermaid's tongue.

On the journey back through the forest, the slimy creatures backed away from the dazzling potion that shone in her hand. The sea-king's palace was deserted and the little mermaid did not dare to look for her sisters to say goodbye. Instead, she picked a flower from each of their gardens before rising up through the blue waters.

It was just before sunrise when she reached the marble steps of the prince's palace. She drank the magic potion, and the pain that burned through her body was so terrible that she fainted. When she awoke, the handsome young prince stood over her, gazing at her tenderly. She looked down at her slim white legs and wrapped her long hair around her body to cover herself.

The prince asked who she was, but she could not answer. He held out his hand to lead her into the palace, and every delicate step she took was like treading on knife-points.

The prince ordered the little mermaid to be dressed in silk and muslin robes and everybody agreed that they had never seen a more beautiful, graceful girl. But then a girl with a beautiful voice sang to the court making the prince smile and clap, and this made the little mermaid sad.

"If only he knew that I have sacrificed my own sweet voice for love of him!" she thought.

When the music began to play for dancing, the little mermaid raised her beautiful white arms, stood on tiptoe and seemed to float across the floor. Although she felt as if she was stepping on daggers, she danced so enchantingly that everyone in the court declared they had never seen anything so lovely. The delighted prince never took his eyes off her and said that he would never part with her – his "little creature from the seas".

They spent their days together, riding through the perfumed forests where the little birds sang amongst the cool leaves. They climbed mountains together until they could see the clouds rolling beneath them. Although her tender feet bled, she only laughed at her sufferings. At night, while other people slept, the little mermaid sat on the marble steps and bathed her poor, burning feet in the cool sea water.

One night, her sisters swam to the surface hand in hand and floated over the water towards her, singing. They told her how much they missed her. Once, in the distance, she saw her old grandmother and the sea-king with his crown on his head, stretching their arms out towards her. But neither of them would venture near the shore.

Each day, she grew fonder of the prince and he loved her as though she were a favourite child. But if he married someone else, she would never have a human soul and would melt into foam the day after his wedding.

"Do you love me best of all?" she asked with her eyes.

"Yes, I love you best of all," replied the prince, "and I know that you love me. You remind me of a girl I once saw, but who I

The Little Mermaid

"'I KNOW WHAT YOU WANT,' SAID THE SEA WITCH"

shall never meet again. I was shipwrecked and thrown ashore near the convent of a church where some young girls were saying their prayers. The youngest of them found me and saved my life. She is the only other one in this world that I could love, but she belongs to the convent. You have almost made me forget about her."

"He doesn't know that it was I who carried him across the sea and saved his life!" thought the little mermaid. She sighed deeply, and would have cried if mermaids were able to shed tears. "I will take care of him and love him, and sacrifice my whole life to him."

One day the prince came to tell her that she must get ready for a journey. "My parents wish me to meet a princess in another kingdom. They want me to marry her, but that I can never do since I do not love her. But at least I must obey my parents by going to visit her," he said. "I cannot marry my love in the convent, but if I am ever forced to choose a bride, it would be you." And he kissed her rosy mouth.

A few days later, they boarded a magnificent ship and set sail for the neighbouring kingdom where the princess lived. At night, when everyone was asleep, the little mermaid sat on deck in the moonlight and gazed into the clear waters. She thought she could see her father's palace and her grandmother staring up at the ship. Then her sisters appeared on the surface and gazed at her sadly. She waved and smiled to tell them she was happy.

Next morning, the ship arrived in the neighbouring king's capital city. For many days, the prince and his court were entertained with feasts and balls. The princess had not yet arrived as she was travelling from far away.

When at last she arrived the prince could not believe his eyes.

"It is you!" he cried, "You are the girl who rescued me from death on the shore!" The princess blushed and nodded. "I am so happy!" said the prince to the little mermaid. "My dream has come true. You must be happy, too, for you love me better than anyone!" The little mermaid kissed his hand and felt as if her heart was about to break.

The church bells rang and the heralds rode far and wide to announce the coming wedding. The little mermaid, dressed in gold silk, held up the bride's long train, but she hardly noticed the magnificent ceremony. After the bishop's blessing, the bride and bridegroom went on board ship, where a gorgeous scarlet tent lined with beautiful purple cushions had been prepared for them.

The ship sailed smoothly across the calm sea and, when darkness fell, coloured lamps were lit and the sailors danced on deck. The little mermaid remembered her first visit to the human world and how she had watched the party on the boat. She twirled round and round in the dances, gliding and darting in the air like a frightened swallow – never had she danced so enchantingly. The agony in her feet was terrible, but worse by far was the agony in her heart. She knew this was the last night she would breathe the same air as the prince, for whom she had sacrificed everything, and the last night she would be able to gaze into the starry sky or into the depths of the sea. When everyone had gone to bed and all was quiet, the little mermaid stayed on deck and waited for the sun to rise. She saw her sisters rising from the waves with pale faces and saw with astonishment that they had cut off their hair.

"We wanted to save you so we gave our hair to the sea-witch," they explained. "She gave us this knife. Take it and plunge it into the prince's heart so that his blood sprinkles your feet. They will turn back into a fish's tail, and you will be a mermaid once more!"

The little mermaid lifted the scarlet curtain of the tent and saw the sleeping prince and his bride. She bent to kiss the prince's beautiful head, then looked at the sharp knife. The prince was murmuring his bride's name in his sleep. The little mermaid held the knife tighter. She raised it high above her head, and flung it far out into the water. She looked at the prince one last time, and threw herself into the sea where she felt her body dissolve into foam.

The little mermaid could still see the ship's white sails and the bright sun. High in the air, there were clouds of transparent, floating spirits. She felt herself gently rising out of the foam and saw that she had turned into one of the floating spirits in the air.

"We are the daughters of the air," they said. "We try to bring comfort and help to the world. We fly to hot countries and fan the air to bring coolness, and we blow the scent of flowers into refreshing breezes. Like you, we were born without a soul but, after three hundred years, if we have done enough good in the world, we are given one. During your time among human beings you suffered terribly, but behaved so unselfishly that now you have become a spirit of the air. Come and join us, and in three hundred years you will have a soul."

The little mermaid lifted her eyes to the sun and, for the first time, they filled with tears. She saw the prince and his bride looking for her and then gazing at the pearly foam, as if they knew that she had thrown herself into the waves. She kissed the bride's forehead and fanned the prince with a cooling breeze and flew up to join the other air spirits on a rosy cloud sailing high in the sky.

"In three hundred years, I will rise like this into the heavenly kingdom beyond the stars," she thought.

"Perhaps it will be sooner," whispered the air spirits. "For every day that we meet a good, loving child, a year is taken away. But for every naughty child, each tear of sorrow that we shed adds another day."

The Little Mermaid

"Dancing over the floor as no one had yet danced"

THE WILD SWANS

Long ago there lived a king with one pretty daughter, named Elise, and eleven very handsome sons. Their mother, the queen, had died when they were still quite small, but now they were growing up the king began to feel lonely, and wanted to marry again. Although the new queen was beautiful, she was really a witch. She disliked her stepchildren and treated them very badly.

First, Elise was sent far away from the palace to live with a poor old woman deep in the forest, and then the queen told terrible lies to make the king cold and suspicious towards his sons. But they were his sons and he wouldn't send them away. After a while, the wicked queen's patience ran out and she cursed them, turning them into eleven snow-white swans.

The Wild Swans

"Fly away! Fly from this kingdom and never return!" she cried, as the eleven swans rose into the air, wheeling away on great white wings.

All night long they flew above the forest looking for Elise, until they found the little cottage where she lay sleeping. They tapped at the windows with their beaks and flapped their wings loudly, but she did not wake. As the sun rose they gave up and soared above the clouds, heading for the silver ocean shining far away in the distance.

As Elise grew older she became prettier than ever. As she played in the little cottage garden, the wind would whisper to the roses, "Is anyone more beautiful than you?" And the roses would answer, "Only Elise." She was a kind child too, and when the breeze fluttered the pages of the old woman's prayer-book asking, "Is anyone kinder than you?" it replied, "Only Elise".

When she was fifteen years old, the king asked Elise to return to the palace. When the wicked queen saw her lovely fair skin and shining golden hair she shook with hatred and rage. She wanted to turn Elise into a swan like her brothers, but she was afraid of angering the king. Instead, she decided to prepare a magic bath for Elise. She threw in three slimy toads, chanting, "Sit on her head and make her stupid. Sit on her brow and make her ugly. Sit on her heart and blacken it."

As soon as Elise got into the bath, one toad perched on her head, one on her brow and one on her heart. But her goodness and kindness were stronger than the queen's evil magic and they immediately vanished, leaving only three red poppies behind.

The furious queen pretended to rub soothing oil into Elise's skin, but instead she smeared evil paste all over her, and rubbed ashes into her face and hair. When Elise was presented to the king she looked so ugly and dirty that he sent her away again, saying, "This filthy wretch cannot be my daughter!"

Poor Elise ran away and walked all day across the fields towards the forest, longing for her eleven brothers. She felt sure that they too had been driven away.

When night fell, Elise slept on the soft moss and dreamed of her brothers and her dead mother.

In the morning the sound of birdsong and rippling water woke her. She walked through the trees and bushes to a beautiful, clear lake and bent down to drink.

When she saw her dirty face in the water she was frightened at first. Then she undressed and swam in the lake, washing away the paste and the ashes until she was clean and pretty once more. She dressed and tidied her hair and went deeper into the forest to find food. She found an apple tree and ate until she felt better.

"Everything will be all right," she told herself.

Next day, Elise met an old woman carrying a basket of berries and asked her if she had seen eleven princes.

"No," said the old woman, "but yesterday I saw eleven swans with gold crowns on their heads. They were swimming in the river close by. Come and I'll show you."

The old woman led Elise to a narrow, winding river and the girl set off along its banks, following it until the river flowed into the rolling sea. There she wandered along the shore wondering what to do. It was then that she spied eleven white swans' feathers caught up amongst the seaweed. She sat down on the shore holding them, dreamily watching the ever-changing sea.

As the sun began to sink into the sea, Elise saw a ribbon of eleven white swans with crowns on their heads flying towards the land. She ran and hid behind a bush to watch. As soon as the sun dipped below the horizon, the swans' feathers fell away and Elise's brothers stood there. She ran towards them and flung herself into their arms, calling

The Wild Swans

their names. When they had all stopped laughing and crying with joy, the eldest prince spoke: "While the sun is in the sky we are condemned to be swans, but the moment it sets we become human again. We live far across the sea, but once every year we make the journey back to our native land. It is a dangerous journey, and it takes two long days to make. There is only one small rock that juts up above the waves between there and here, and we must sit on it all night, crowded together for safety with the wind and waves crashing over us. We are allowed to stay in the land of our birth for just eleven days each year, and we have two days left before we must fly off again. Come back with us, dearest Elise."

"I will," said Elise, "and I must try to break your spell." At sunrise, the princes became swans and flew away, all except for the youngest who stayed with Elise, nestling his head in her lap. In the evening, the others returned and at sunset they became human again.

"Tomorrow we must fly home again," said one. "But we can carry you between us across the ocean." The brothers and sister spent the night weaving a large, strong net and at sunrise the princes turned back into swans and flew into the sky, carrying the sleeping Elise.

All day long they flew onwards, but they were slower than usual because of the weight of the net. Towards evening, dark clouds appeared. Elise began to feel frightened and looked for the rock. The sun began to sink and a storm blew up, with flashes of lightning illuminating the sky. The sun had almost disappeared completely when the swans suddenly swooped down towards a little rock that looked no bigger than a seal's head. As the last glimmer of sun sparkled on the horizon, the brothers' feet touched the rock and they became human again, standing arm-in-arm around Elise without an inch to spare.

They clung together all night while the storm raged around them, saying their prayers to give themselves courage. By dawn the storm had died away, and the swans flew up into the still air carrying Elise.

Ahead she saw fantastic shapes in the sky, a huge castle of shining towers among ice-covered mountains, and gigantic flowers in forests of waving palm trees. The swans told her that it was the fairy Morgiana's cloud-castle and that no human could ever enter. As Elise gazed at it, it seemed to turn into twenty ornate churches and then it changed into a fleet of sailing ships.

At last they saw real land, and by sunset Elise and her brothers were sitting on a rock in front of a large cavern. That night, Elise fell asleep praying for the knowledge to break the spell. In her dreams she entered Morgiana's castle, and the fairy herself appeared looking just like the old woman in the forest who had told her about the swans.

"Your brothers can be saved," said the old woman. "But only if you are brave enough and strong enough. Pick the stinging nettles that grow around the cavern. They are the same nettles that grow in churchyards. They will sting you terribly but you must not stop. Crush them into fibres with your bare feet, and don't stop however much they burn and blister you. Weave the fibres into eleven long-sleeved shirts. When you put them over your brothers' heads the spell will be broken. But remember one thing above all others – from the moment you begin this task you must stay silent or your brothers will die."

Elise awoke and the first thing she saw were stinging nettles like those in her dream. At once, she set to work. The nettles burned her delicate hands and feet but she did not care. The princes were amazed and frightened that she would not speak to them, but they realised she was trying to save them. After working all day and night she had finished one shirt.

As she started work next day, the sound of a huntsman's bugle startled her and she picked up her bundle of nettles and ran into the cavern. Within minutes, the cavern was surrounded by barking dogs and a group of huntsmen led by a king.

The Wild Swans

"The whole day through they flew onward through the air"

"What are you doing here, lovely maiden?" asked the handsome young king. Elise said nothing and hid her hands so the king could not see the blisters that covered them.

"Come with me," he said. "I will dress you in silver and gold." And he lifted Elise up onto his horse and rode away to the palace.

When the ladies-in-waiting had bathed her and dressed her in silken robes, the silent Elise looked more beautiful than ever. The king fell in love with her and wanted to marry her, but his chief minister believed she was a witch. The king showed Elise to a little room decorated like the cave, with the bundle of nettles and the finished shirt lying on the floor. "I thought it would remind you of the cavern," he said. Elise smiled and kissed his hand.

Elise grew to love the kind king and longed to tell him about her brothers, but she did not dare. By now, six shirts were finished but all the nettles had been used up. So, that night, Elise crept out of the palace and through the dark alleys and lonely streets to the churchyard. She didn't know that the king's suspicious minister was following her. In the moonlit churchyard a circle of witches danced among the tombstones. Holding her breath, and saying a silent prayer, Elise picked the burning nettles.

When the minister told the king all that he had seen in the churchyard, the king refused to believe him. He loved Elise far too much to believe that she could be an evil witch. But before long all his ministers were telling him not to be blinded by love but to see for himself. So, with a heavy heart, the king decided to watch Elise closely, and soon began to wonder why she spent the night all alone in the little room.

At last, Elise had one more shirt to make but once more the nettles had been used up. This time the king followed her to the churchyard. He took care not to be seen, but when he saw the circle of witches among the graves he felt sick at heart. It must be true.

His beautiful Elise must be one of them. Next day, Elise was tried and sentenced to be burned at the stake. They threw her into a dark dungeon, but at least they left her the nettles and the ten finished shirts. Gratefully, she carried on with her work.

As the sun was setting, she heard a swan's wing rustling against the window of her dungeon. Her youngest brother had found her and she cried with joy to see him. He went to find his brothers, and just before dawn the eleven princes appeared at the palace gate asking to see the king. But by the time the king arrived, the sun was rising and the eleven swans flew away.

At midday, the townspeople poured into the square to see the witch being burned. Elise was pulled along in an old cart with the ten shirts at her feet and her busy fingers working frantically to finish the eleventh. Suddenly, eleven wild swans swooped down and landed in the cart, flapping their wings as if to protect her. The crowd fell silent and whispered, "It is a sign from Heaven! She must be innocent!"

As the executioner approached, Elise threw the nettle shirts over the eleven swans. In an instant, eleven handsome princes stood before the crowd — but the youngest one had the wing of a swan because Elise had only managed to make one sleeve for his shirt.

"Now tell them of my innocence!" cried Elise, fainting into the arms of her brother.

"She is no witch!" said the eldest prince, and he told the whole magical story. As he spoke, every stick on the bonfire took root and burst into flower, and the air was filled with the scent of roses.

The king picked one perfect red rose and pressed it to Elise's heart. She woke and looked into his eyes with a smile of happiness. The king promised Elise they would never be parted again, and that she should become his queen.

THE MARSH KING'S DAUGHTER

The storks tell their little ones many stories about the moor and the marsh where they live. The younger ones enjoy little stories such as "Kribble-krabble, plurry-murry," while the older ones prefer more exciting stories about the adventures of their family. Of the two oldest and longest stories that have been handed down, we know the one about Moses, who was left on the bank of the river Nile and was found by the king's daughter. As we know, Moses became a great man and a prophet.

But you might not have heard the second story. It has been handed down from mother stork to baby stork for thousands of years and each time it has been told it has become better and better. Now we'll tell it best of all.

The first pair of storks to tell the story made their summer nest on the roof of a wooden castle owned by a Viking. The castle was built next to the wild moor of Wendyssel. The moor was in the circle of Hjörring, high up in Skagen, in the north of Jutland. Legend has it that, many years before, the land was covered by the sea, but that the seabed rose up and formed the moor. The moor stretched for miles and miles in all directions and was surrounded by wet marshland, swamps and rough land covered with blueberries and stunted trees. The moor is still there today and is called the "wild moor" because it is always misty. Until seventy years ago wolves still roamed the land.

The land looked the same thousands of years ago as it does today. The reeds were just as tall and had the same long leaves and bluish-brown feathery plumes. The birch tree stood with its white bark and its loosely hanging leaves. Even the creatures that lived there dressed the same; the fly in its dark, velvety cloak, and the stork in its black and white outfit with bright red stockings. The people dressed differently, but they met the same fate if they dared step onto the marsh; they would sink down into the great kingdom below, ruled by the Marsh King. We know very little about the Marsh King's rule, but maybe that is for the best.

The Viking's castle was three storeys tall and it had watertight stone cellars. On the roof, the mother stork was hatching her eggs and looking forward to the arrival of her young ones.

One night, the father stork came home very worried. "I've got something terrible to tell you," he said to the mother stork.

"Don't worry me, I have to keep calm while I'm hatching the eggs or something bad might happen to them."

"I have to tell you," he said. "The princess – the daughter of our host in Egypt – has travelled here to the moor, but she has disappeared."

"Oh, tell me what happened, quickly – don't keep me in suspense when I'm hatching."

"Well, she thought that the flowers on the moor would heal her sick father, so she flew here dressed in swan's feathers. She came with two of the other princesses who fly here every year in swan's feathers to renew their youth and beauty in the sacred water."

"You're babbling!" exclaimed the mother stork. "The eggs will get cold, stop keeping me in suspense."

"I was keeping watch," said the father stork, "and tonight when I went into the reeds I saw three swans. But there was something strange about them – they weren't real swans, they were just swan's feathers!"

"Enough about feathers! What about the princess?"

"Well, you know the lake in the middle of the moor?" continued the father stork. "The three swans were sitting on the tree stump near the reeds. Suddenly, one of them threw off her feathers and I saw that it was the princess from the house we nest on in Egypt. I heard her tell the others to look after the feathers while she dived under the water to find the flower. The others picked up the feathers, but then they flew off with them! As they flew away they cried, 'Dive down into the water! You'll never see Egypt again!' and they tore the feathers into a thousand pieces and let them flutter to the ground like snow. Then the two cruel princesses were gone."

"That's terrible!" said the mother stork. "I can't bear to listen! What happened next?"

"The princess wept and her tears fell onto the tree stump. But it wasn't a tree stump after all – it started to move. It was the Marsh King who rules under the moor. He rose from the ground and I saw that his arms were like long, thin branches. The poor princess was terrified. She tried to run away across the slimy ground, but it wouldn't take her weight and she sank down and down until big black bubbles rose from the slime. As the bubbles burst, both the princess and the Marsh King disappeared. Now the princess is buried deep in the wild moor and she'll never return to Egypt with the flower!"

"Stop telling me such terrible things!" cried the mother stork, "I'm sure the princess will escape, or someone will come to find her."

"But I'll go every day to see if anything happens," said the father stork. And he did.

A long time passed. One day, the father stork saw a green stalk shooting up from the moor ground. After a little while, a leaf unfolded and grew bigger and bigger until a bud appeared. As he flew overhead one morning, the bud burst open and in the centre there was a beautiful little girl. She looked just like the Egyptian princess, and the father stork realised that it must be the Marsh King's daughter.

"I can't leave her lying there," he thought, "but my nest is full already. The Viking's wife would love to have a child, though … I know! People always say that storks bring children, so that's what I'll do. She'll be so happy!"

So the father stork picked up the child and flew to the castle. He placed the baby gently next to the Viking woman as she slept, and then he hurried home to tell his family what had happened.

"…So, the princess isn't dead because she must have given birth to the child," he said.

"Okay, that's wonderful. Now think about your own family," said the mother stork, "we need to start preparing for our flight to Egypt – the cuckoos and nightingales have already set off. The young ones have been practising their flying and I think they're ready."

When the Viking's wife woke up she was overjoyed to find a baby girl beside her. She cuddled it but the baby cried violently and struggled until she had cried herself to sleep. When the baby was sleeping she looked beautiful and tranquil, and the Viking's wife was happy.

The Viking's wife knew that her husband would be returning home soon, so she started to prepare the house. The maids hung up the tapestries, polished the shields and arranged the cushions. They built a fire in the hearth, ready to be lit when the Viking returned. By nightfall, the Viking's wife was very tired and she quickly fell asleep.

When she awoke, the baby had vanished. She searched the room for the child, but all she found was a great big ugly frog. She was so horrified that she grabbed a heavy stick and was just about to hit it when she noticed that it was looking at her with large, mournful eyes. She could not bring herself to harm it, so she opened the window to let it out. But at that moment a golden ray of sunshine fell on the frog, and, before the woman's eyes, its ugly great mouth shrunk to a small red one and its limbs stretched to become beautifully symmetrical. It was no longer an ugly frog, but the beautiful baby girl.

"Am I dreaming?" asked the woman.

She kissed and hugged the baby, but it struggled and fought like a wild cat.

Meanwhile, the Viking was on his way home. But the wind was blowing against him and so his journey was long and slow.

After a few nights, the Viking's wife decided that a terrible spell must have been cast upon the child. In the day, she was as beautiful as an angel of light, but her temper was savage and wild. But at night she became an ugly frog with large sorrowful eyes. You see, by day

The Marsh King's Daughter

"They were returning home, richly laden with spoil, from the Gallic coast"

the girl had the body of the Egyptian princess but the Marsh King's temper, and by night she had the body of the Marsh King but the kind heart of the Egyptian princess.

The Viking's wife longed to find someone who could break the spell. She spent her days weeping with sorrow, and yet she still cared for the child. She feared that her husband might find out the terrible secret and leave the baby out on the road to die, and she knew in her heart that she could not allow it. She decided that the Viking must only ever see the child in daylight.

One morning, the Viking woman heard a rushing noise overhead. She saw above her that the storks had started their journey south. The young storks had practised hard and they flew as lightly as the wind.

At that very moment the sound of trumpets rolled across the moor; the Viking and his warriors had landed and were returning home. They brought with them hoards of treasure from the French coast, where the villagers sang, "Save us from the wild Northmen!"

The men came home in high spirits. The fire was lit and a great feast began. Many guests were invited and each received a gift. The minstrel sang a song, which praised the men's warlike deeds and bravery. Every line of the song ended with these words:

"Goods and gold, friends and foes will die;

Every man must one day die.

But a famous name will never die!"

And with that the men would hit their shields and hammer the table.

The Viking's wife wore a silk dress and beautiful golden bracelets, covered in amber beads. The minstrel sang that she had brought the richest treasure of all to her husband in the form of a beautiful daughter. The Viking was delighted with the girl, especially with her savage ways. He declared that she might grow up to be a heroine of the land, as strong and determined as any man that ever lived. She would be so brave that she would not even flinch if her eyebrows were cut off with a sword.

The feast was magnificent and continued through the night.

Later that year, the Viking set sail again. His wife stayed at home with the girl, and soon she began to love the frog with its gentle eyes and sorrowful sighs more than she loved the pretty child that bit her and beat her all day.

The thick autumn mists that covered and devoured the leaves of the forest had descended on the moor. Winter was fast approaching. Snow flew down and covered the land in its thick blanket, and the sparrows took up home in the empty storks' nest.

The storks were now in Egypt, where the sun shone every day and the flowers bloomed all year round. Stork-pairs sat resting on the slender towers of the many Egyptian temples. They built their nests in the fallen pillars and temple arches of long-forgotten cities. Palm trees lifted their leaves like sunshades and the great pyramids cast their mighty shadows over the vast desert, where the ostrich ran and the great marble sphinx lay half buried in the sand. The water of the Nile had receded and the muddy river bed was covered in frogs. It was such as glorious sight that the young storks thought they must be dreaming.

"Yes, it's wonderful. It's always like this in Egypt," said the mother stork.

The young storks were so excited that they wanted to explore.

"There's nothing else to see," said the stork mother. "Beyond here there is lush green forest, but the branches are so intertwined that only an elephant can force its way through. The snakes there are too big and fast for us. If you go into the desert you'll get sand in your eyes and you might get caught in a storm. It's best to stay here with me where there are frogs and locusts to eat."

So they stayed. The parents rested in their nests and cleaned their feathers. The young female storks pranced around in the reeds, peeking at the other storks and making friends. Meanwhile, the young male storks fought in the mud. The days were hot and sunny and full of fun. But inside the Egyptian's palace life was not as happy.

The rich lord of the palace was lying on his divan in the luxurious great hall. The walls were so brightly coloured that he looked as if he was lying in the centre of a tulip. His limbs were so stiff and weak that he looked like a mummy. He was on the verge of death. All his friends and family had gathered, and they were worried that his beautiful young daughter, who had flown off in the swan's feathers, had not arrived home with the moor flower to heal him. "She's dead!" the two cruel princesses had cried when they returned home without her. They had made up a long story about what had happened:

"We flew high up in the air, but a hunter spotted us and shot an arrow at us. It struck her and she sank to the ground, singing her farewell song as she went. She sank down, a dying swan, into the woodland lake. We laid her under a weeping birch tree by the shore of the lake. Then we had our revenge: we lit a fire in the swallow's nest that sat under the hunter's thatched roof. The house burned to the ground and the hunter was taken by the flames. The glare of the fire shone across the sea near the weeping birch under which she sleeps."

Then the two girls wept. When the father stork heard their story he clapped his beak with anger.

"Lies!" he cried, "I'd like to peck them with my beak!"

"But then they would hurt you," said the mother stork. "Think of yourself and of your family, and forget everything else."

"Tomorrow I'll sit and listen when the wise men gather to discuss the Egyptian's health. Maybe they'll uncover the truth."

The wise men gathered and talked for hours about the Egyptian man. But the father stork could barely understand a word they said.

But there was one thing the father stork could understand: everyone in the land, wealthy or poor, thought that it was a great tragedy that the man was dying, and everyone hoped that he would recover. The people had searched and searched for the flower that would cure him, but none of them had found it. They had read books, consulted the twinkling stars in the night sky, and they had read the weather and the wind for signs. All that the wise men could say was, "Love creates life and will restore a father's life," which even they did not understand. They said it again and again, until it became simply, "Love creates life." They tried to turn it into a recipe, but they did not know how. Finally, they decided that only the princess could have helped her dying father, because it was her that loved him most. It was her that a year ago had entered one of the great pyramids and visited the tomb of a great pharaoh. It was there that she had had a vision that she must restore her father's health by bringing home a lotus flower from the bottom of the deep lake in the north. Eventually, they decided that, as the princess would not return, all they could do was wait to see what happened.

"I'd like to take those two feather cloaks away from the cruel princesses," said the father stork that night, "so that they can't fly to the moor and cause any more trouble. I'll hide the cloaks so that the princesses can't find them and I'll wait until there's a good time to use them."

"Where will you hide them?" asked the mother stork.

"In our nest in the moor," he answered. "We'll take turns carrying them on our journey home. One of the feather cloaks should be enough for the princess, but it's better to have two just in case."

"You won't get any reward," said the mother stork. "But, you're in charge, so we'll do what you say."

In the Viking's castle on the moor, the little girl had been named Helga. With every year that passed the wickedness in her grew. The storks continued to make their autumn journey to Egypt and back again, and before long Helga was a beautiful girl of sixteen. She looked beautiful on the outside, but inside she was harsh and cruel. She enjoyed sacrificing animals just to see the blood flow from them.

But the Viking was so bewitched by her beauty that he did not see the wickedness inside her, and he did not know how she changed with the daylight.

Helga rode her horse without a saddle as it galloped around the land, and she would take off her clothes and leap from the cliff into the sea and swim to meet the Viking's boat when it neared home. She even cut her longest lock of hair and twisted it into string to use on her bow.

The Viking's wife was strong and brave, but compared to her daughter she looked feeble and timid.

Out of malice, Helga would sit on the edge of the well and dive into it, just to scare her mother. She would emerge again as a frog, dripping with water from the dark, murky depths.

But there was one thing that Helga could not control: the evening twilight. When twilight came she became quiet and thoughtful, and she listened to people's advice. Then she longed to be with her mother. When the sun went down, the transformation happened and she turned into a large, ugly frog. Her sad eyes returned and all she could do was utter a hollow croaking noise that sounded like the muffled cry of a dreaming child. Then the Viking's wife would cuddle her and look into her eyes, so that she forgot how ugly she was and loved her.

"I almost wish you were always a frog," the woman would say, "because when you are a girl you are so wicked."

The Viking's wife wrote many charms to try to break the evil spell, but none of them worked.

"I can hardly believe that she was once small enough to fit in the centre of a water-lily," said the father stork, one day. "She looks just like her poor Egyptian mother, who we will never see again. Year after year I have flown to and from Egypt, but the princess has never once given me a sign that she is still alive. Every year, when I arrive here before you to repair the nest for your return, I spend a whole night flying over the lake searching for her. But she is never there and so those two feather cloaks that we brought with us from Egypt have never been used. It took us three journeys to get them here and now they just line the nest. If the Viking's house were to burn down, the feathers would go with them."

"And our lovely nest would be destroyed too!" said the mother stork. "But you think more about those feathers and the princess than about us! I just hope that none of our children will be shot down by that wild girl's arrow. Helga doesn't know the consequences of her actions. She should remember that we have lived here longer than she has, and that every year we have been good and given the Viking an egg, a young stork and a feather as we are supposed to. I'm angry with Helga and with you. You should have left her lying in the water-lily to die."

"You don't mean that," said the father stork, "you're kinder than you make out."

With that he flew away, with his head stretched forward proudly. The sun glistened on his feathers.

"He's the handsomest stork there is," said the mother stork to herself, "but I won't let him know that!"

Early in the autumn, the Viking came home with masses of treasure and some prisoners. Among the prisoners there was a young Christian priest who preached against the gods of the north.

There had been much talk in the castle about the Christian faith spreading across the land. Even Helga had heard of the man who had sacrificed his own life for mankind, though she had ignored it along with most things she heard. She only understood the word "love" when she was crouched in the corner of her room in the form of a frog. But the Viking's wife had heard the story too, and she felt moved by it.

After their last voyage, the men had told everyone in the castle all about the incredible stone temples that had been built to worship the Christian God. Among the treasure that the Vikings brought home there were some gold bottles filled with unusual fragrance; these were the incense vessels that the Christian priests swung as they stood at the altar.

The young Christian priest had been tied up and locked in the castle cellars. The Viking's wife thought that he was as beautiful as Balder – the most beautiful of Viking gods – and she felt sorry for him. Helga, on the other hand, believed that he should be tied to the tail of a bull, which should be let out to run round the fields.

"Then I would let the dogs out – over the moor and across the swamp! That would be a sight for the gods!" she cried.

But even the Viking would not condemn the priest to such a horrible death.

He decided that the priest would be killed on the sacrificial stone, for being an enemy of the northern gods. This would be the first time that a man had been sacrificed there.

Helga begged her father to let her sprinkle the priest's blood at the sacrifice, and she began sharpening her glittering knife. Suddenly, one of the castle's savage dogs ran past and she thrust her knife into its side, just to test the knife's sharpness. The Viking's wife looked sadly at the cruel, wild girl. When night came, and Helga had exchanged her beauty for a gentle soul, the woman spoke of the sorrow that was deep in her heart.

The ugly frog stood there with its big brown eyes and listened so carefully that it seemed as if it understood the woman's words.

"I've never told my husband what I've had to go through," said the Viking's wife. "My heart is full of sorrow; for the love of a mother is more powerful than I had ever imagined. But you have never felt love – your heart is wet and cold like the plants on the moor."

The frog trembled: the words had bridged the gap between its body and its soul. Tears started to well in its eyes.

"A terrible time will befall us both," said the Viking's wife. "It would have been better if you'd been left in the road and the night wind had lulled you to sleep."

The Viking's wife wept bitterly and walked away. The frog crouched alone in the corner. The room was silent except for a stifled sigh that came from its mouth – from Helga's mouth. A new life was beginning in her heart.

She hopped forward and pushed open the heavy door. It was as if something powerful inside her was giving her strength. She picked up a flickering torch and crept into the cellar. The prisoner was asleep and when he awoke he saw such a large, hideous frog that he believed it must be a spirit. She cut the ropes that were tied around his hands and feet, and then she stood beside him.

He made the sign of the cross and said, "Who are you? Why do you appear as a hideous animal when your heart is so kind?"

The frog-woman beckoned him to follow her. She led him out to the stables and she pointed to a horse. The two mounted it and galloped into the night.

The priest felt how loving and merciful the creature was, despite its ugliness. He believed that it must be God who had sent this monstrous spirit. He prayed and sang, and Helga started to tremble. Was she cold, or did the words hold some kind of power over her? She wanted to stop the horse and get off, but the priest held her with all his strength and continued to sing. He hoped that his words would break the spell that had turned her into this ghastly creature. The horse galloped faster than ever and the sun rose, flooding the land with its brilliant light. The frog changed its form and there appeared the beautiful, but wild, Helga. The priest was horrified when he saw her; the spell must be even more terrible than he had thought. He jumped off the horse, as did Helga. She drew her knife and lunged at the astonished priest.

"I'll get you!" she screamed, and they struggled. But the priest seemed to have an invisible power and he was able to hold her still. Suddenly, the roots of the old oak tree above them curled around Helga's feet so that she could not move. The priest sprinkled her face with water from a nearby spring and commanded the evil spirit in her to leave. He blessed her, but nothing happened because Helga had no faith in her heart.

But the priest would not give up. He continued to bless Helga until his words overpowered her. She dropped her hands and gazed at him with frightened eyes and pale cheeks. To her, the priest looked like a mighty magician with great knowledge of secret arts; he seemed to speak in a dark language and to be making strange signs in the air. Helga shook when he signed her with the cross, and then she sat with her head bowed like a tame bird.

The priest told her how she had appeared to him as a hideous frog and freed him. He explained that as long as she was under the spell she would be more of a prisoner than he had been, but that he would release her. He would take her to Hedeby, to the holy man Ansgarius, and in the Christian city the spell would be broken. But he would not let her sit at the front of the horse.

"You must sit behind me," he said. "Your beauty comes from evil and I am frightened by it, but I am sure that it will disappear when you have faith."

He knelt down and prayed. It was as though his prayer turned the woodland into a holy church; the birds sang like a choir and the wild flowers were as fragrant as incense.

Helga was in a daze; not awake but not asleep, as if she were a sleepwalker. The priest lifted her onto the horse and tied two branches together to make a cross, which he held up high as they rode on through the forest. The wood became thicker as they rode, until it was just a wilderness.

The priest spoke about faith and Christian love as he tried to lead the poor lost girl towards the light.

People say that raindrops can wear away hard stone, and that the waves can smooth the rough edges of the rocks. In the same way, the dew of mercy smoothed Helga's rough surface and the harshness inside her. It was not obvious at first, but the priest had sown the seed of faith and kindness, which would one day blossom in Helga. Just as children repeat their mother's words without knowing what they mean, and only begin to understand them as they grow older, Helga did not yet realise the importance of the priest's words.

They rode on through the dense forest. As it grew dark, they came across a group of thieves who dragged Helga and the priest to the ground. The priest tried to defend them using Helga's knife, but one of the thieves swung an axe at him. The priest sprang to the side and the axe hit the horse's neck and killed it. At the sight of blood, Helga awoke from her trance and threw herself on the animal. The priest tried to defend her, but one of the thieves swung his hammer on the priest's head with an almighty blow. The priest sank to the ground, dead.

The thieves seized Helga and rode off. As the sun went down, she transformed once again into a frog. A huge white-green mouth spread over her face, her arms became thin and slimy and her webbed fingers spread out like fans. The thieves were terrified and let her go, so she hopped into the bushes. The thieves believed that the frog must have been an evil spirit, so they hurried away.

The moon shone over the earth, and Helga crept through the bushes in her frog-like form. She stood beside the body of the priest and the carcass of the horse. She let out a croak like a child bursting into tears, and then she wept. She sprinkled them with water, but they were dead and finally she understood. She could not bear the thought that soon the wild animals would come to devour the bodies, so she dug a grave for them as well as she could with her webbed hands. Before long, her hands were torn and bleeding, and she could dig no more. She washed the priest's face again and covered him with green leaves and stones, which she then covered with moss until the grave hill was secure. The sun rose and Helga stood there in all her beauty with bleeding hands and tears flowing – the first to have ever touched her cheeks.

It was as if two personalities were struggling inside her. Her body trembled and she looked around as if she had awoken from a terrible dream. She climbed to the top of a tree and held on tight.

The Marsh King's Daughter

"He knelt down and prayed fervently"

She stayed there in the silent solitude of the wood all day, like a startled squirrel. The butterflies flapped around her and the bees went about their work, while all the other winged creatures buzzed around. The wood was silent except for the noise of the animals. No one noticed Helga except a flock of crows that flew above her. They hopped close to her, but when she looked at them they flew away. They could not understand what she was, and neither could she.

When twilight came, the transformation happened again. Yet this time Helga's eyes glistened with beauty even greater than when she took the form of a beautiful girl. Her eyes were pure and lovely, and they showed her deep feelings and the gentleness of her heart. Her eyes overflowed with tears and the precious drops were a wonder to see.

On the grave hill there lay the cross that the priest had made. Helga lifted it up and planted it in the ground. Then she drew the same cross in the sand around the grave. As she drew the sign the webbed skin fell from her hand like a torn glove. She washed her hands in the spring and was amazed at the pale skin that appeared. She made the sign of the cross in the air and then her lips trembled. She spoke God's name, which the priest had told her during their ride through the forest. The frog skin fell from her and she was a beautiful girl again, but she was so tired that she fell into a deep sleep.

At midnight, Helga awoke. In front of her there stood the dead horse. It was beaming and full of life. Close beside it stood the priest – as beautiful as Balder. But he seemed to be standing in a flame. His eyes had a look that was so powerful and just, and so piercing, that it penetrated every corner of Helga's heart. She trembled as though she were being judged. She remembered every good deed that had ever been done for her and every loving word that had been spoken. Finally, she understood that it had been love that had kept her in the wood. Helga realised that in the past she had been cruel. She now knew that everything that was happening was because of God. She bowed down before Him, He who knows every thought in every heart, and she confessed that she was not perfect. Then the priest spoke: "Daughter of the moor," he said, "you came from the earth, and from the earth you shall rise. I come from the land of the dead. You, too, will pass through the valleys between the mountains where mercy and wholeness live. I cannot lead you to Hedeby and baptise you until you have burst the spell of the water on the wild moor and freed your mother. You must show that you are good before you can be blessed."

He lifted her onto the horse and gave her a golden censer, like the ones she had seen in the castle. The wound in the priest's head shone like a crown. They rode through the air, over the wood and the hills where the old heroes and their horses lay, and the figures rose up and stationed themselves ready for battle. Each wore a halo and a cloak, which floated in the night breeze. The dragon that guards buried treasure lifted its head and looked at them. The gnomes and spirits of the wood peeked from the hills and from the fields, and they flittered around with red, green and blue torches, like sparks in the ashes of burnt paper.

The priest and Helga fled up to the wild moor and hovered over it. The priest held the cross up and it gleamed like gold. He spoke in prayer and Helga joined in as he sang hymns, like a child joining in with its mother's song. She swung the gold vessel and the incense swept over the moor. The reeds and grass blossomed and plants sprung from the ground. Everything that was alive lifted itself up and water-lilies spread out into a carpet of flowers. Helga thought she saw herself sleeping in the calm waters, but it was her mother: the Marsh King's wife, the princess from Egypt.

The priest ordered that the sleeping woman be lifted onto the horse, and then the three glided from the moor to more stable land.

The cock crowed in the Viking's castle. The ghosts faded away until just the mother and her daughter stood looking at one another.

"Am I looking at myself?" asked the mother.

"Is it my own reflection I can see in front of me?" exclaimed the daughter.

And then they hugged. The mother knew in her heart that this was her daughter.

"My child! The flower of my heart, the lotus flower from the deep waters!" And she hugged the girl again and wept. The tears were like a baptism of new life and love for Helga.

"I came here in a cloak of swan's feathers," said the mother, "and I took it off here, but then I sank deep into the black slime. A force pulled me deeper and deeper until I was asleep, and my dreams hovered all around me. I dreamt that I was back in the pyramid, but the weeping birch willow was always in front of me and then it became a mummy. I couldn't tell if it was the Egyptian pharaoh or the Marsh King. He seized me and I thought I was going to die. When I woke up, a little bird was sitting on my chest, twittering and singing. It flew up towards the dark surface of the lake, but I was still held to it by a green band. I understood its words, 'Freedom! Sunlight! To our Father!' it said. Then I thought of my own father and sunny Egypt, of my life and love, and I loosened the green band and let the bird soar away to its Father. Since then I haven't dreamt at all. I was in a long, deep sleep until your harmony and fragrant incense set me free."

Where had the green band gone that tied the mother's heart to the bird's wings? Only the stork had seen it; it was the green stalk from the beautiful flower, the cradle of the child that had become a beautiful girl, and who had now been reunited with her mother.

While the two were hugging, the father stork flew above them.

Then he flew back to his own nest. He brought out the swan feather cloaks and threw one onto each of the women so that the feathers closed around them. They soared into the air like two white swans.

"Now you can understand me," said the father stork. "I'm glad you came tonight because tomorrow we are flying to Egypt. Mother stork always said that the princess would help herself! At dawn we'll set off together. We'll guide you so that you don't get lost."

"And the flower that I was supposed to take home," said the Egyptian princess, "is flying by my side in the swan's feathers. I am bringing with me the flower of my heart, as the prophecy told."

But Helga would not leave until she had seen the kind-hearted Viking woman one last time. Helga remembered all the woman's tears and her kind words, and she felt as though she loved the Viking woman most of all.

"Yes, we'll go to the castle," said the father stork, "mother stork and the young ones are waiting for us there. They'll be so excited!"

When they arrived at the castle everyone was asleep, except for the Viking woman. She was worried about Helga, who had vanished with the priest three days before. She knew Helga must have helped him to escape because her horse was missing from the stables, but she couldn't work out how it could all have happened. The woman had heard the priest talk of miracles, and, as she lay there thinking about him, she fell asleep. She dreamt that she was lying awake on her bed and that outside a storm was drawing near. She heard the roar of the waves and she knew that the northern gods were about to fall. The war-trumpet sounded and the gods, dressed in their armour, rode over a rainbow to fight their last battle. It was a terrible hour.

The Viking woman saw Helga crouching nearby in her hideous frog form, and she hugged her as the battle passed overhead. The sky was going to burst, the stars would fall and everything would be swallowed up in a sea of fire. But she knew that a new heaven and earth would be formed and that God would reign. The priest rose up to Him, and the Viking woman kissed the forehead of the frog. Then the frog skin fell off and Helga stood in all her beauty, more gentle and lovely than ever before. She kissed the Viking woman's hands and thanked her for the kindness that she had sown in her. Then Helga rose in the form of a magnificent swan, spread her white wings and soared into the air.

The Viking woman awoke and she heard the same roaring noise outside. She knew the storks would be leaving and thought that it must be their wings that she could hear. She went outside and saw them flying overhead in large circles. But in front of the well, where she had often sat with Helga, there were two white swans gazing at her with knowing eyes. She remembered her dream, which had felt so real, and thought of the priest and Helga as two swans. At that thought, she rejoiced.

The swans arched their necks and flapped their wings as if they were greeting her. She opened her arms and felt the truth all around her. She smiled and stood deep in thought.

Then the storks set off. "We can't wait for the swans any longer," said the mother stork, "if they want to join us, they will have to come now."

And so they set off together for Egypt. The birds flew over the Alps towards the Mediterranean.

"Egypt!" sang the Egyptian princess as they reached the shore.

They flew faster and faster at the sight of land.

"I can smell the mud and the frogs," said the mother stork, "and it's making me hungry."

"The storks have arrived," said the Egyptian people in the wealthy households on the banks of the Nile. The royal lord still

The Marsh King's Daughter

"She was once a more beauteous maiden"

lay on his bed, not alive and not dead, but waiting and hoping for the flower from the moor in the north. His friends and family had gathered once again.

Suddenly, the two beautiful swans flew into the room, accompanied by storks. The swans threw off their feathers and two beautiful women stood in their place. They were almost identical, and they both bent over the pale old man. When Helga bent over her grandfather the colour rushed into his cheeks and his eyes grew brighter. Life came back into his limbs and he stood up, cheerful and healthy as his daughter and granddaughter hugged him.

The house was filled with joy. The wise men wrote down the story of the two princesses, and of the flower of health. Meanwhile, the stork father told the story to his young ones.

"Now they'll appreciate you, there's no doubt," whispered the mother stork.

"But I haven't done anything," replied the father stork.

"You've done more than anyone else. If it wasn't for you, the two princesses would never have returned to Egypt and cured the old man. I'm sure they will honour you, and the honour will be passed from you to our young ones, to their young and so on."

"I can't tell the story as well as the wise men can," said the father stork, who had overheard the wise men talking, and was now telling his own family. "They told it so wisely that they were honoured and given presents."

"And what did they give to you?" asked the mother stork. "Surely they didn't forget to honour the most important person of all! The wise men did nothing but talk."

Late that night, when everyone else was asleep, Helga stood on the balcony and looked at the stars. She thought of the Viking woman in the wild moor, of her gentle eyes and the tears she had wept for the hideous frog-child. That same hideous frog-child now lived in Egyptian splendour, under gleaming stars, on the bank of the Nile. She looked at the water and thought of the glory that had shone from the priest's wound when they had flown across the moor. She remembered the words that had come from the great fountain of love that embraces all of mankind.

Day and night, Helga thought about how happy she was. She knew it was a miracle that had brought her here and given her such bliss. But she thought about her happiness so much that she forgot to think about God. Her happiness made her courageous, and she was unfolding her wings for a great flight. Then she saw two ostriches running around in a circle. She had never seen such clumsy creatures, with such ineffective wings, and in her mind she heard the Egyptian legend of the ostrich.

Once, ostriches were beautiful and glorious birds with strong, large wings. One day, one of the largest birds of the forest said to the ostrich, "Shall we fly to the river to drink, God willing?" And the ostrich answered that they should. At dawn they flew high up towards the sun, which gleamed like the eye of God. They flew higher and higher, the ostrich flying highest of all. Proudly, he flew straight at the light, boasting of his strength and not thinking about God, or saying "God willing". Suddenly, an avenging angel drew the veil off the flaming sun and the heat scorched the proud ostrich's feathers so that he fell to the ground. Since then he has not been able to fly, but instead has had to run feebly on the ground. The story is a warning not to forget to say, "God willing".

Helga bowed her head thoughtfully, and she realised that she must never forget about God.

In the spring, when the storks were leaving again for the north, Helga took off her gold bracelet, scratched her name on it and hung it around the father stork's neck. She asked him to take it to the Viking woman so she would know that she was safe, and had not forgotten her.

The bracelet was heavy around his neck, but he believed that the Viking people would think that storks brought with them good fortune, so he bore the load.

"You lay gold and I lay eggs," said the mother stork, "but they don't appreciate either of us."

"But you and I know that we have done good deeds, and that is enough," replied the father stork.

"You can't hang that around your neck," retorted the stork mother, "and it won't give you fine weather or a good meal."

A little nightingale was sitting on a tamarind tree nearby. It would soon be heading north, too. Helga had often heard it singing sweetly when she lived on the moor. She asked the nightingale to fly to the beech wood in Jutland, where she had built the grave hill, and ask all the other birds to build their nests near the grave. That way, their sweet songs would sound over it for the rest of time. The nightingale flew away and time flew, too.

In autumn, the wealthy and handsome Prince of Arabia came bearing many gifts. When the stork family arrived in Egypt it was a very joyous time in the household; Helga and the prince had been married that day and she was dressed in silk and shining jewels. The bride and groom sat side by side between Helga's mother and her grandfather. But Helga was not looking at the groom; she was looking at a gleaming star that shone down from the sky.

Although the storks were tired, they flew straight down to the veranda where the wedding feast was being held. Helga had asked that a mural of the storks be painted on the wall, to illustrate her story.

"That's wonderful," said the father stork.

"But it's not enough," replied the mother stork.

When Helga saw them she stood up and went out to the veranda to stroke their backs. The pair bowed their heads, and even the young ones felt honoured by the princess's welcome.

Helga looked at the star; it seemed to glow brighter and purer than ever. In front of her floated the spirit of the Christian priest, who had come down from heaven to join the wedding feast.

"The glory of heaven is greater than anything on Earth!" he said. Helga begged the priest to show her the kingdom of heaven, just for a moment. So he took her up into the splendour, where she heard voices that beamed so brightly that words cannot express it.

"We have to go back now, people will be missing you," said the priest.

"Just one more look!" she begged, "Just one more wonderful minute."

"We have to go, otherwise all your guests will have gone."

"Just one more, this is the last one – I promise."

And then Helga stood on the veranda. But the marriage lights had gone and the lamps in the hall had been put out. The storks were not there, nor were the guests or the groom. Everything had been swept away in those few minutes.

A wave of dread came over her. She walked through the empty hall where she found strange warriors sleeping. She opened the door to her bedroom, but through the door there was a garden instead. The sky was red and it was morning.

Three minutes in heaven and the whole night had passed.

Then Helga saw the storks and she called to them in their own language. The father stork flew to her. "You speak our language," he said. "What do you want? Why are you standing before me, strange woman?"

"It is I – Helga – don't you remember me? We were speaking here three minutes ago."

"No, you must have dreamt it," replied the father stork.

"No," she continued, "you must remember the Viking's castle and the journey across the vast ocean to get here."

The father stork blinked his eye and said, "That's an old story that I heard from my great-grandfather. There was once a princess here from Denmark, but she vanished on her wedding night many hundreds of years ago and never returned. You can read about it in the monument in the garden where there are marble sculptures of two swans. Behind them you are carved in marble, too!"

And there it was. Helga saw it and understood, and she sunk to her knees.

The sun burst through the clouds and Helga's spirit flew up into heaven. Her body crumbled to dust and all that was left where she had stood was a lotus flower.

"Well, that's a new ending to the story," said the father stork. "I hadn't expected that, but I like it."

"But what will the young ones say?" asked the mother stork.

"Yes, you're right, that's the important point," he replied.

The Marsh King's Daughter

THE GARDEN OF PARADISE

There was once a prince who read all the books that he could find. He learned everything he wanted to know except for one thing: how to find the Garden of the World.

When the prince was little, his grandmother had told him that the flowers in this magical garden had petals that tasted of sweets, with centres full of honey. Even better, whoever ate them instantly knew all the history, geography and mathematics there was to know and didn't need to go to school! When the prince became a man, he understood that this story was not really true, but still he wanted to know the real secrets of the Garden.

One day when he was walking in the forest the sky went black and a heavy rainstorm started. Suddenly he heard a roaring noise and saw an enormous cave in which an old woman was roasting a deer on a spit.

"Come and dry yourself by the fire," she said to the soaking prince.

"There is a strong wind blowing in here," said the prince.

"It will get worse when my sons come home," replied the old woman.

"You are in the Cavern of the Winds. My sons are the Four Winds of Heaven and they fly to the four corners of the earth. Ah! Here is one of them now." And the North Wind blew in, spreading icy air and snowflakes all around.

He wore a bearskin jacket and a sealskin cap. Shining icicles swung from his beard and hailstones showered from his shoulders. Snowflakes were scattered in all directions.

"What are you doing in the Cavern of the Winds?" he shouted at the prince.

"He is my guest," said the old woman fiercely, "and if you are rude to him, I'll put you in your bag!" And she pointed at four large bags hanging on the wall.

The North Wind became quieter, and told them what he had seen on his travels.

"I saw whalers hunting in the Arctic Ocean on my way to Bear Island. What a splendid island – half-thawed snow, sharp stones, and the skeletons of sea-cows and polar bears! I blew into the mouths of baby birds in their nests and taught them to shut their beaks! Best of all, I drove icebergs towards the whaling fleet and made it hurry south as fast as it could!"

Next, the West Wind whirled into the cavern with a rush. He was clutching a heavy wooden club and looked like a wild man.

"I have come from the forests," he said, "where no humans

live. I swooped down into the river and soared upwards carrying a rainbow. I saw wild buffalo swimming and flew with a flock of wild ducks. I danced on the prairies, I stroked the horses and I raised howling storms!" He kissed his mother so hard that she almost stumbled and fell to the ground.

In flew the South Wind, dressed in a turban and swirling desert robes.

"It is cold in here!" he complained, throwing wood on the fire. "I have been in Africa, running races with the ostriches and rolling in the desert sands. I met a caravan of camels and buried them in the Sahara. When I puff away the sand, the sun will bleach their bones!"

"What a terrible thing!" said his mother. "Into the bag with you!" And she grabbed the South Wind and put him inside where he wriggled and squirmed but could not escape.

"Your sons are certainly very lively!" said the prince, as the East Wind blew in.

"I have come from China where I danced in the temples to make the bells ring and whirled through the towns, raising dust storms," he announced proudly.

"So that is where you have been," said his mother. "I thought you told me you were going to the Garden of the World."

"I shall go there tomorrow," said the East Wind. "It is a hundred years since my last visit."

"A good thing too," said his mother. "It will improve your mind. When you are there, drink from the Fountain of Wisdom and bring me back some of the water."

"I will," said the East Wind. "Now, if you let my brother out of the bag, he can tell me about the phoenix. The fairy in the Garden of the World will want to hear news of him."

The Garden of Paradise

"SHE TOOK THE PRINCE BY THE HAND AND LED HIM INTO HER PALACE"

When the old woman let the South Wind out of the bag he gave the East Wind a palm leaf, saying, "The phoenix gave me this. On it he has written the story of his life, which spanned one hundred years, for the fairy to read. It tells of how he sat on his nest and then set it alight, burning himself to ashes before being reborn."

"Is the fairy beautiful?" asked the prince. "And where exactly is the Garden of the World?"

"If you want to go, I will take you," said the East Wind. "It is on the Island of Happiness, where the Angel of Death cannot go."

When the prince awoke next morning, he found himself already on the East Wind's back riding high above the clouds. He gazed down in wonder at the green fields and tiny houses. Soon they were over the sea, whipping up the waves and blowing the sailing ships along.

They flew on across wide plains and through deep forests. As they crossed the Himalayan mountains the East Wind said, "Soon we shall reach the Garden of the World." Now the prince could smell the scent of spices and pomegranates, and saw grapevines in the fields. Swooping down, they landed on soft grass among bright, nodding flowers.

"Is this the Garden of the World?" asked the prince.

"Not yet," replied the East Wind. "Do you see that cave over there, half-hidden by hanging vines? That is the way through. Wrap yourself in your cloak because it will be as cold as ice inside."

They flew through vast chambers, with ceilings as high as a cathedral, past strange rock sculptures and along tunnels so narrow they had to crawl on all fours. A beautiful blue light beckoned them onwards.

Then the rock above them became hidden by mists until they emerged in a beautiful land. The cool air was scented with roses and

The Garden of Paradise

a clear river, sparkling with gold and silver fish, ran by. Scarlet eels swam slowly along the river bed, flashing blue sparks, and orange water-lilies floated on the surface. A bridge of marble lacework stretched over the water, leading to the Island of Happiness and the Garden of the World.

The East Wind lifted the prince onto his arm and carried him across the river. They floated among beautiful palm trees, festooned with colourful flowers and hanging creepers. Birds with feathers like rainbows perched in the trees, singing the sweetest songs the prince had ever heard, whilst in the grass below them a lion and a tiger played together like kittens. When the prince reached out to stroke a peacock's tail he found he was touching a plant. It was the most amazing and wonderful place he had ever seen.

The fairy of the garden appeared, dressed in shining robes and with a gentle, beautiful face. The prince presented her with the phoenix's palm-leaf and she read it with sparkling eyes. Then she led him into her palace, which was like being inside the petals of a glowing flower. Through every window he could watch a scene from earth's long history as if it was happening then and there. He saw the mountains of the earth being formed millions of years before. They went into a vast hall with transparent walls, on which hung thousands of living portraits. And in the very centre stood a tree with drooping branches laden with golden apples. This was the Tree of Knowledge. From its leaves red dewdrops fell like tears of blood.

"Climb into the boat," said the fairy. "It does not move, but rocks gently while the world glides past." They saw snow-capped mountains, dark forests, ancient temples, exploding volcanoes, burning deserts and arctic wastelands, and they heard the cries of animals, music playing and voices singing.

When the Northern Lights lit the sky like a huge firework display the prince was delighted.

"Can I stay here for ever?" he asked.

"You can, but only if you do not want the forbidden fruit," replied the fairy.

"I promise never to touch the fruit on the Tree of Knowledge," replied the prince.

"Think carefully before you make that promise," said the fairy.

"The East Wind flies home tomorrow and you can return with him. If not, you must stay here for a hundred years. The time will pass quickly, but it is long enough for temptation to overcome you. Each evening I shall ask you to follow me, but you must refuse. Every day, the temptation will grow stronger and you will find it harder to refuse, but you must do so. I sleep beneath the Tree of Knowledge. If you lean over me while I am asleep, I will be forced to smile and you will kiss me. Once you do that, the garden will sink into the earth and be lost to you for ever."

"I shall stay here," said the prince. So the East Wind kissed him goodbye saying, "Be strong and we shall meet again in a hundred years!" Then he flew away and left the prince.

"Now our dances must begin," said the fairy. "At sunset, when I am dancing with you, I shall say, 'Come with me.' Do not do it. Each time you refuse you will grow stronger."

The fairy led the prince into a ballroom made of transparent white lilies. A golden harp played in the centre of each flower, and beautiful fairies danced and sang sweetly. When the sun set, the golden sky filled with all the colours of the world. A feeling of happiness and bliss came over the prince. The ballroom wall seemed to vanish and the Tree of Knowledge appeared before him in such streams of light that his eyes were dazzled. In a sweet, tempting voice,

The Garden of Paradise

" 'Now we will begin our dances!' cried the fairy"

the fairy cried, "Come with me!" Immediately, the prince forgot his promise and rushed towards her. The perfumed air grew sweeter, the music sounded clearer and a thousand voices sang, "We must know everything! Man rules all the earth!"

"I must follow!" said the prince. "Surely nothing bad will happen. I will only see the fairy sleeping!" The fairy pushed aside the drooping branches of the Tree of Knowledge and disappeared from sight. The prince followed her and found her asleep at the foot of the tree. As he leaned over, she smiled in her dreams and he kissed her on the lips.

At that instant, a huge clap of thunder shook the air and the frightened prince saw the beautiful garden collapse in ruins and plummet into a deep, black hole. At the bottom, he could see the garden twinkling like a faraway star. The prince fell forward, fainting. When he awoke, cold rain beat on his face and a freezing wind howled about him. The Mother of the Winds sat next to him, and she was angry.

"How could you be so weak? And on the very first evening!" she said. "If you were my son I would put you in the bag!"

"He will learn his lesson soon enough," said the Angel of Death, who sat on the prince's other side. "But I will give him the chance to make up for his weakness. If, when his time comes to die, he has been good I will take him up to a beautiful garden among the stars. But if he is evil I will sink him lower even than the Garden of the World."

ORIGINAL PAINTINGS

Harry Clarke's original illustrations for Hans Christian Andersen's *Fairy Tales* at the National Gallery of Ireland

This book includes reproductions of the 11 Harry Clarke original paintings held at the National Gallery of Ireland. High quality photographs of these pictures have been digitised and reproduced with the stories they accompanied in the original 1916 book, published by Harrap. These are shown again over the following pages.

The remaining colour illustrations and all black and white drawings have been scanned from a first edition of the original 1916 edition. Despite modern scanning methods, the quality of these images, especially those in colour, cannot match the photographs of the NGI collection, as the printing techniques used in 1916 were unable to reproduce paintings with the fidelty that is possible today.

Each colour plate in the 1916 edition was printed on a different paper to the text pages of the book, then pasted by hand into place in the book. Some of the black and white images were also printed and bound separately into the book.

The original 1916 text has been edited for a modern audience and four stories have been omitted in this edition: *The Galoshes of Fortune*, *The Old House*, *The Butterfly* and *What the Moon Saw*.

Hans Christian Andersen

Frontispiece

From *The Elf Hill*

From *The Nightingale*

Original Paintings

From *The Garden of Paradise*

From *The Wild Swans*

From *The Snow Queen*

Hans Christian Andersen

From *The Travelling Companion*

From *The Tinder Box*

From *The Swineherd*

Original Paintings

From *The Shepherdess and the Chimney-Sweeper*

From *The Little Mermaid*

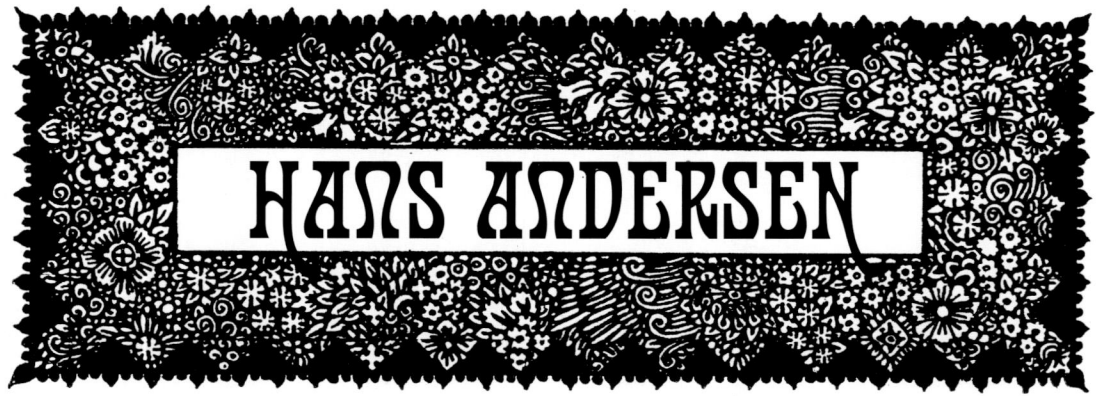

The life of Hans Christian Andersen
(2 April 1805–4 August 1875)

Hans Christian Andersen was born in the quiet provincial town of Odense in Denmark. His father was a very poor shoemaker and Hans read the books he kept in his workshop. As a boy, he was fascinated by stories and would often go to listen to the old women in the workhouse telling the traditional tales that had been handed down over the years by word of mouth. There was also a theatre in Odense that he would visit to watch travelling actors perform.

When he was 14, he left Odense to try his luck in the Royal Theatre in Copenhagen, the capital city of Denmark. He wanted to act and dance, and to write plays for the theatre. Although he was unsuccessful at first, the director thought he showed promise and sent him to school. Hans Christian Andersen always worked very hard but he never made much money. However, he made some wealthy friends and they made sure he never starved. His poverty gave him the ability to write about the hard conditions under which many people lived, while his friends gave him a taste of the glittering society that rich people enjoyed.

By the time Hans Christian Andersen had reached his mid-thirties, his first three novels (out of the six he wrote in total) had become popular, particularly in Germany and Sweden. When his fairy stories were gathered together and published as a book in 1839, he became famous throughout Europe and, indeed, the world.

His fame then spread to Britain and America, where he was seen as one of the most important writers of the time, and his work was translated into many languages. He travelled all over Europe and wrote five travel books. Altogether, he lived outside Denmark for more than nine years. After such freedom, the narrow way of life in Denmark often made him angry, but he kept returning to the country of his birth. He had been born at a time when countries were governed only by kings and emperors, but during his lifetime, he had seen the middle classes take over government and give the vote to many ordinary people.

Portrait of Hans Christian Andersen by Albert Küchler, 1834

Hans Christian Andersen was a modern, forward-thinking man and encouraged these developments. He also had great sympathy for students and working men, remembering his own struggles when he was young. He wrote plays for the Students' Association and sometimes acted in them with the students. He also spent a lot of time reading and lecturing to the Workers' Association in Denmark.

When he died in 1875, at the age of 70, a guard of honour was formed at his funeral in Copenhagen Cathedral by students and working men.

Acknowledgements

pages 2, 19, 55, 97, 108, 118, 135, 149, 169, 175, 215, 218, 219
Copyright © National Gallery of Ireland

page 223
Portrait of Hans Christian Andersen
Wikipedia Commons

All other images copyright © Teapot Press Ltd

Introductory text, pages 6–13
Copyright © NGI, 2011

Text
Copyright © Teapot Press Ltd, 2011